Death Stakes A Claim

Vikki Walton

CHAPTER ONE

Christie fired the gun until the chamber was empty. Shots rang out, and she hit her target. She dropped the magazine and racked the slide. With her left hand, Christie pushed the button next to her and the paper figure silently made its way toward her like a ghost. She undid the target and handed it to the instructor, who removed her ear protection.

"Great job. You passed. You'll receive your certificate, and then you'll have your license to carry." Christie smiled at the woman but didn't respond. After recent events, Pop insisted she learn how to protect herself. While she'd said she'd take up martial art instruction, Pop responded with a headshake.

"Darlin', I know you want to think the best of people, and I'm glad you do. Unfortunately, there are bad hombres out there, and times have changed. I want you safe and that means carrying."

She'd appeased her father and taken to learning how to shoot like any other instruction. Christie found she had good eye-hand coordination, and it became a fun challenge to hit the center every time. However, she remained cognizant of the power of life and death within this small instrument in her hand. That nugget of fear never left her, and the thought of carrying it with her didn't equate with the life she lived or wanted to live.

"Thanks. I appreciate all your help with form and learning proper procedure." It had surprised Christie to see Lana in the ladies' class; though, it did make sense. Someone with a gun had killed Lana's father, and she had two young children to protect. After her father's death, Lana's mother had returned to the home she'd always known. However, with Lana's kids in school, she'd stuck it out at least until the summer. She was renting the house across the street from Christie's friend, Orchid Merryweather, and while their paths hadn't crossed since her father's death, they would often wave at each other.

Christie set the pistol in the carrier and removed her protective glasses. Her instructor followed suit, and they exited the room. Lana stood there. "How d'you do?"

"I passed. Are you going in?" Christie motioned toward the instructor holding the door.

"Nope. I finished my practice right before you." She held up the target with most shots dead-center and one off to the side. "I missed one. Happened at my test, too. I tried

to get her to let me take it over, but she wouldn't let me."
She stuck out her bottom lip in a mock pout.

"I'm sure you'd have achieved what you set out to do.
Stop a bad guy—or gal." Christie's stomach rumbled as
they walked outside. "Hey, I'm grabbing some lunch. What
d'you say?"

"Sounds good. I have to pick up the kids, so it'd be
great if we do something in Boerne, so I miss any traffic."

Christie responded, "I'm okay with that. Diengers?"

"Works for me. I'll meet you there." She waved to
Christie.

At the café, they ordered their meals and then took a
spot by the brick wall and a bank of windows. Lana ordered
a latte, and she took a long sip. "Ah, just what I needed.
After our mad morning rush to get the kids out the door,
they still missed the bus. The school run left me with

limited time to head over for my college test." She laughed cheerfully. "As you can guess from my rambling on and on, I missed my cup of coffee this morning."

"I'm a coffee gal myself, so I totally get it." Christie took a drink of her water as the waitress appeared and set down their soups and salads. "My goal is to drink more water though."

"Good habit to get into. I need to do that too." They settled into easy conversation over their meal.

After they'd split a dessert, Christie broached the subject. "I hope I'm not being too nosy, and if you don't want to talk about it, let me know. I'm wondering how you're doing and if you're planning on moving."

Lana's face grew red as she struggled to control her grief. She swallowed and wiped a tear rolling down her cheek. "I still can't believe my dad's gone. I even struggle to say he's dead. He was such a good man. Why anyone would want to harm him—"

Christie folded her hands. "I'm sorry, Lana. Evil often hides in plain sight. I'm not sure what I can do, but if you need anything, I'll do my best to help."

"Thanks." Lana sniffed and wiped her eyes with her napkin. "Orchid, the lady across the street, has been bringing me things. She encouraged the kids to do an art project about their grandpa and asked me to join them. I'm amazed that doing something so simple as making a collage of all the things we remember about him could be so helpful. Orchid is—"

"Special?" Christie raised an eyebrow.

Lana chuckled. "You might say that. I struggle with trying to nail down what it is about her. She's eccentric, but empathetic. It's like she can see into your soul and know what you need the minute you need it. She's been a god-send to us; that's for sure." She took a bite of the cake.

"I know what you mean. We're so different, and yet we get along so well."

"Like pieces of a puzzle." Lana laid down her fork and sat back in her chair.

Christie cocked her head. "Interesting way to consider it."

"It's what my dad used to say. Everyone is a piece of a puzzle, and when you meet someone that fits, you sense it instinctively… here." She pointed to her heart. Then sighed. "That's the way he said it was with my mom. So it's no surprise her not wanting to stay. I understand my mom wanting to move back, and to be honest, we needed some space from each other. Two strong women under one roof does not harmony make!"

Christie chuckled. "I'm sure."

"I do miss her—and certainly the help—but this time alone has been good for me and the kids. It was such a shock when my husband died. Mom and Dad were at a loss as to how to help. They'd already agreed to the Texas move, so it made sense for me to come too and start over with them." She exhaled. "Now, here I am, still figuring out what I should do. My next step has to be what's best for my children. I do know that."

"Sounds like you're a good mother. Please, I'm here if you ever just need to talk things out aloud. I'm a good listener." Christie smiled.

"I recognize that. One thing I'm doing is introducing the kids to my dad's father—Mr. Altgelt. It seems funny that he's my grandfather, but it's a family connection here. I admit I struggled at first with wondering if he was to blame in my father's death, but you can look at how this hurt him." She wiped her mouth with a napkin. "He lights up when the kids and I come over. He makes me laugh with all his silly jokes. He's like another puzzle piece I didn't realize was missing."

"I'd be careful calling him Mr. Altgelt. He won't take to that. But I'm glad that you all will get to appreciate one another."

"I don't. He insisted we call him Curtis, but the kids call him Papa, so that's his name now. His face beams when they run to him, calling him that." Lana's phone beeped. "That's my signal to get going so I can get to the school and in line before the crowd grows." She stood. Christie followed her outside, and they walked toward their vehicles.

Lana clicked her key fob to open the door. "Nice seeing you again. Let's go shooting sometime."

"Sure. To tell you the truth, I did it to satisfy my Pop. But it would be good to continue the practice."

"You mean you got your license, but you won't carry a gun?"

Christie shook her head. "Nope." She looked at Lana. "Will you?"

Lana motioned at Christie to come closer to the vehicle before looking left and right. Christie followed her gaze, but other than a car driving by, she spied no one near them. Lana lifted her top slightly. Underneath, she wore what appeared to be a corset with pockets. On her right side, a pocket contained a small pistol.

"Wow, I would have never known."

Lana dropped the top and smoothed it down. "Yep, I love her stuff. Anna Taylor. You should check out her videos. I have one for my dresses and skirts too. I'll get you the info for her company, Dene Adams." She reached over and hugged Christie. "Thanks for listening to me. I hope we'll have more chances to get together." She waved and climbed into the truck. Christie watched as she drove away.

Could she be around someone who carried a gun? Even after taking the lessons, she still struggled about it. Her entire life, she'd lived without carrying a gun. Why start now? While Lana was a small woman—maybe five-feet-two, if that, Christie was a bigger and taller woman. It would seem to make sense she could handle an attacker. Yet, doubts had crept in. Size didn't matter if someone had evil intent. She'd long recognized people carried concealed, but she enjoyed being oblivious to it. No doubt in her mind now. She was officially back in the state of God, Guns, and Grit.

Christie pulled keys from her purse and hit the key fob to unlock her truck. She started the truck when her phone went off.

"Hey, Pop. What's up?"

"Erik's back in town."

"Pop, I'm on my way home. Let's talk about it when I get there."

Christie shivered at the prospect of Erik back in town again. Erik swore he hadn't started the fire in their barn. Had it been a coincidence and something—or someone—else had sparked the blaze? Because Jess had attacked Erik to defend her, it left Christie in a terrible position. She didn't want to get the teenager in trouble, so they'd dropped the trespassing charges. Erik returned to Dallas, and she'd assumed she'd seen the back of him. So why return now? There was only one reason. Something had made him think that his stake in his grandfather's property was at risk.

She banged her hand on the steering wheel. Lana. Of course. She was one of Kurt's heirs. If Erik could persuade her to get her mother to agree to his plan to sell the property, he'd win easily. From her conversation with Lana, it sounded like Curtis continued to invite her and the kids over. Who could have found out and told Erik?

She pulled over into a parking lot entrance and braked. The Websters. Peering over her shoulder, she made sure the road was clear before pulling a U-turn. She didn't understand what she would do once she got to Webster Realty, but she felt an obligation to Lana and her kids to ensure they didn't have to deal with the likes of the Websters or Erik.

She parked and strode toward the building that housed the realty company. Inside, it took her a minute to survey the new interior decoration. Before, the décor had been typical Texan. Now the walls displayed modern paintings, and in place of the wood receptionist desk stood a shiny modern partition with a large, etched Webster Realty logo on the front. The receptionist was also new to Christie. The thirties-something woman wore an expensive-looking suit and held up a French-manicured finger to Christie as she spoke on the phone.

After ending the call, the woman with cat's eye-glasses and a bold red lip, spoke. "May I help you?"

From the quick surreptitious glance up and down, Christie noted the woman's instantaneous judgment. In dressing for the shooting range, Christie had thrown on a pair of faded blue jeans, a tank top, and an old flannel shirt that screamed comfort over chic. "I was wondering if Emma was in."

"I'm sorry. She's out right now. And you are—?"

"Christie Taylor. We've been discussing a possible sale of a portion of our property." She struggled to determine how she'd get the information she needed. "Um, is Tyler here?"

"Mr. Webster is also out right now."

Christie noted the change of inflection in the woman's voice and how she'd accorded Tyler respect, but not Emma. Interesting.

"I'd like a quick look in the conference room. There's a house plan I'm interested in and I'd like to get the name." She forced a smile for the woman.

"Of course. Follow me, please." The woman flicked her straight black hair over her shoulder and sashayed in front of Christie in a tight, short skirt and a pair of expensive red-soled three-inch stilettos.

Who wears that kind of outfit in Boerne?

She stood to the side of the door as Christie entered to find the wooden conference table replaced by a glass-top model with a chrome base. A magnificent piece of modern sculpture featured where the large wooden owl had once stood. The pictures also bore new contemporary frames, and Christie acted as if she were seeking a specific one.

"Wow. The office has really changed. It may take me a minute to locate the picture… so no need to wait."

"No problem." The woman called out, "Albert, can you come here, please?"

Albert appeared in the doorway. She tilted her head and smiled at him. "Will you please stay here while I return to my desk?"

Christie stifled a chuckle. She'd never understood the need to flirt to get what you wanted, but by Albert's face, it was working.

After the receptionist left, Christie spoke. "Albert, I wanted to ask about the status on the property with Curtis Altgelt. Any news there?"

"Not that I know of." He crossed his arms and leant back against the doorframe. "Why?"

So he wouldn't give out any information either. "Is Erik Stewart back in town? Is this true?"

"Where'd you hear that?"

Christie figured it would be easier to be direct. "If you must know, I want to ensure my safety as well as that of the teenager that's in my charge right now. Erik trespassed, and Jess fought him off from harming me." Even though Jess had recovered from his fight with Erik physically, sometimes Christie glimpsed a hint of fear at strange noises. She wanted Jess to feel safe with them.

Albert moved away from the door. "From what I picked up, you all attacked him and lied about him starting a fire in your barn. Eric thinks you tried to frame him for starting the fire."

"That's insane."

"Not my issue." He shrugged.

"I just want to learn why he's back. Maybe to see Beatrice."

"Beatrice? What do you mean?"

Now she had his attention. "They're an item. I saw them kissing." She waited for his response, which was immediate.

"What?"

"Looks like we're both surprised. You want to tell me why he's here now?"

Albert's face and neck grew splotchy red. "You need to leave. I can't tell you anything about a client."

"Fine. But you tell Erik he better not show up at our place. I have a gun now, and I'm not afraid to use it." Why had she said that? She had no intention of using a gun.

He stepped toward her. "That sounds like a threat. I'd be careful if I were you."

Christie pushed past him into the hall and toward the front door. Outside, she took deep breaths to steady herself. She wanted to get home to Pop, and they needed to speak to Curtis.

CHAPTER TWO

Christie hurried home where Pop sat in a rocker on the porch. Mutt and Jeffrey, the two labs who were his shadows, lay at his feet. As she opened the truck's door, the pair bounced up and ran to Christie before she exited the truck. They danced around her legs until she gave each of them a pat on the head and scratches behind the ears. "Okay, okay. Enough already. Let me get by." She went over to the porch, the boys following at her heels.

"Pop, who told you that Erik was back in town?"

He patted the rocker beside him. "Curtis. You know everyone knows everything here. Someone saw him and then told someone who told someone else, and there ya have it. Everyone knows Erik's been trying to get his hands on the Altgelt property and, as we've now seen, will do anything to get it."

She sat down and Mutt laid his head on her lap, his gaze imploring for more strokes, "I wonder if the reason that he's come back is that Kurt Matthew's wife left town, and Lana is getting to know Curtis." Christie patted Mutt's head while Jeffrey circled three times and plopped down in a warm patch of sunlight.

"That explains a lot. Curtis has been turning down my invites to go play dominoes in the afternoons with the guys." He stroked his beard. "That's the way, all right. A woman comes into the picture and everything changes."

"Pop, Lana isn't a 'woman.' I mean, she is—oh, you know what I mean. She's been taking the kids over there, and they are enjoying the time spent with him. I know Curtis has to get lonely in that big, old, rambling house."

Unlike the tiny house Pop had, Curtis and his wife had always wanted a big family, so they'd built a six-bedroom home.

The house comprised two living areas for the family and the front room, where the ladies would gather for tea. A large dining room connected the two rooms. The family room was next to the kitchen and breakfast area. The space was always warm and cozy and often reminded Christie of her friend, Kandi's home in Carolan Springs, Colorado. Curtis spent most of his days in that gathering space and had moved from the master bedroom to the smaller second master right off the kitchen. They'd built that room for guests and older family members, and it had its own adjoining bathroom with a shower. When Erik and Nick had been young, the large master had been a quiet retreat. This had changed to a hub of medical activity when Curtis's wife had succumbed to cancer and she'd begged him to let her die at home, surrounded by her own things instead of a sterile hospital room. Curtis had moved to the other room and, after her death, never returned.

"I'll speak with Curtis when Lana's not there. I think she'd planned on taking the kids over today after school." Her phone rang. "Speak of the devil—Hello, Curtis." Christie listened and nodded her head. "Sounds good. We can be over in a bit." She disconnected the call.

Pop shifted in his chair and rubbed his arm. He still had twinges of pain from the accident when a truck side-swiped him. "What'd he say, and why's he calling you and not me?"

"Maybe it's because he knows that I carry my phone with me all the time. Where's yours?"

"It's somewhere in the house."

"My point, exactly." She stood up and stretched. "He's invited us to come over for supper."

"That's different. But works for me. Let me go get ready." He waved off her hand of assistance.

When they arrived at Curtis's, they saw a new addition to the large, old oak next to the house. Someone had strung a large tractor tire up with a long rope, and Lana's children were playing on it. Their squeals and laughter as they pushed off with their feet was a welcome sound.

Christie pulled her truck up next to Lana's. Curtis stood up from a wooden bench in the tree's shade and waved at them. He ambled over. Pop clapped him on the back. "I see whatcha' been up to. I could've helped you."

"With that bum shoulder?" Curtis guffawed. "Nah, I got Jess to help me. You shoulda' seen him climb that tree—like a monkey. No way I'd a done it."

Lana appeared on the porch, wiping her hands on a towel. She waved at them and called out, "Y'all hungry?"

Christie smiled at how quick Texas word usage snuck into people's speech. She turned to the men. "Will you nice gentlemen please escort me?" They each crooked an arm, and she laced hers through theirs. Inside the house, smells emanating for the kitchen made Christie's mouth water. "Whatever it is sure smells good."

In the kitchen, a roasted chicken, browned to perfection, sat on the counter resting. Covered pots most likely held a medley of vegetables and potatoes. Yeast rolls were in the oven. After Lana had brought glasses over to the table, she added a pitcher of tea and a sugar bowl.

"Sorry, we don't do sweet tea where I'm from, so you must add your own sugar." Lana set the bowl down with some teaspoons.

"That's sacrilege." Pop winked at her, and she smiled back.

Curtis was the one to bring up the subject. "So I figured it would be best if we all got together and worked on what I'm calling our Erik problem. He reached out to Carole, Lana's mother, about getting the property sold. She told him to stuff it and that she had no need for the property and were it to go to anyone, it would be Lana." He pursed his lips, then sighed. "That brought Erik back to us. I don't know if he's seen Lana and the kids coming out here or someone told him, but I've noticed things not right again. They'd calmed down some, and I had thought I wasn't losing my mind. But they're happening again. Items not where they should be. Things like that." He took a swig of tea. "I've even told Lana that it may not be safe for her and the kids to come visit me. But she'd have none of that."

Christie glanced over at Lana, wondering if Curtis knew she carried a gun. It wasn't her place to say anything, so she didn't. She didn't want to spend all their time talking about Erik. "I saw that you have staked out another barn area that's a bit bigger and further back."

"Yep, Jess and I walked it out, and last weekend, Mike came home from Midland and helped orient it. He made some good suggestions. That Mike's a smart guy. Any woman would be lucky to have such a hard worker." He twisted his mouth.

Christie rolled her eyes. Was Curtis trying to set Mike up with Lana? Lana's kids could use a father, and Jess would be a great big brother, but Mike was her age. Lana needed someone younger. "Speaking of—where is Jess? Is he coming for supper here? I sent him a message, but he hasn't responded yet. Should I call him?"

"He's working on a project at school. Extra credit. Said he'd stop by later." Curtis rubbed his hands. How much longer for them rolls to be done?"

Lana looked at the timer. "Almost. A few minutes and I'm making gravy to go with them."

Curtis covered his heart and pretended to swoon.

Christie was about to chide him about him never doing that for her cooking when Lana's children rushed into the room. Their faces beaming and red from exertion, they ran over to Curtis and grabbed him in a bear hug. "Papa! Papa!" They yelled in unison.

The little girl, a spitting image of her mother, beat her brother to the punch. "We saw an owl in the tree."

The boy nodded his head, his eyes as big as saucers. "It looked right at me!" He shivered with delight.

Curtis stuck out his neck and lowered his voice so that the children craned to listen. "Yep, he comes pretty much around dusk and hangs out in that tree for a bit. Then he goes hunting for mice and bunnies in the field."

"What! I don't want the bunnies to get hurt." The little girl teared up.

Curtis hugged her. "I'm sure the bunnies outrun the owl. You know it can only fly." He winked at Lana.

"Oh, right." The little girl hiccoughed. She turned to Christie and cocked her head. She pointed. "I know you."

"No pointing. It's got a nail in it," Curtis and Lana said. They caught each other's eye and laughed.

Christie stuck out her hand. "I know. You've seen me visiting my friend across the street."

"I like her. She lets me make a mess and doesn't even get mad or anything." The boy plopped on the floor.

"I don't think we've been formally introduced. What's your name?"

The girl twisted her body and tightened her mouth before speaking. "Mommy says to not talk to strangers."

"I agree with your mommy. My name's Christie. Christie Taylor. You tell me your name, and then we won't be strangers."

She shot her mother a look to see if that was okay, and Lana nodded. "Allie."

The boy jumped up from the floor. He bowed. "I'm Trey."

Allie hopped from one foot to the next. "He's not Trey. That means three. He has my daddy's name. Robert. But Mommy called him Bobbie. He had to go to Heaven to help the angels."

"I'm sure you miss him though."

Allie nodded, and tears formed in her eyes. Lana rushed over and gave her a hug, wiping her tears and kissing each cheek. "Go wash your hands, and you can help set the table. You too, Trey. Scoot." The pair rushed off in a bundle of energy.

Lana perched on the edge of a chair. "Some days it's harder than others." She looked at Christie. "I'm sure you know."

She nodded. "Grief's a shadowy tormentor that strikes at will." Christie remembered how many families whose loved ones were under her hospice care would invite her to a celebration of life and they all said something similar. A picture. A song. Anything could set off a flood of emotion. Having lost her mother as a teenager, things like the smell of jasmine or a song still affected Christie from time to time. It would be a long healing process for Lana, Allie, and Trey.

After Curtis said grace, they enjoyed the meal, and the kids kept them entertained with imaginative stories. After supper, Allie and Trey moved to the front room to finish their reading assignments. The adults sat around the table, discussing generalities.

"So, as much as I hate to bring it up, what about Erik?" Curtis grasped the oak table, his rough hands showcasing years of hard labor.

"He hasn't contacted me yet, so what do you think he'll say?" Lana folded her hands.

"I'm sure it'll be something on how you can get rich quick by helping him divide the land and sell it." Pop turned to Christie. "Why don't you bring her up to speed on what we've been dealing with for the last year?"

"I don't think it's been that long, but sure seems like it." Christie then recounted how the Websters had been adamant about securing land to build the development. She shared how she'd seen the plans that showed they planned to build a lot more homes than what they'd told them or Curtis. After getting a nod from Curtis, Christie also shared about Curtis's near-death accident out at the fence line and that it was suspicious. "We still don't know who dug the hole and set up the rock cairn, but I believe it was either Nick or Erik. Whether they only meant to get Curtis out of the picture or to kill him, we'll never know."

Lana gasped. "I'm so glad they found you. I wouldn't have been able to meet you, or the kids meet their great-grandpa." Tears sprung to her eyes. "I don't know what's the matter with me. I cry all the time now." She bit at her lip and struggled for composure.

"Understandable. And no need to explain. You've been through a lot in your short life. But I'm the lucky one, all right. God's given me a great gift in you all." Curtis took her tiny hand in his rough worn ones. "I never got to know my son, but it's because of him I now have you, Trey, and Allie to love." He squeezed her hand. "All things work to the good."

"So what's the plan? Wait and see what Erik does?" Christie searched their faces. Heads nodded.

"He inherits Nick's share. Even though it's way out in the backfield, he may have found a loophole on getting to it. It gives me a bit of worry."

Pop stood up. "Come on Curtis. Let's take a walk out back. I need to stretch my legs after that mighty fine dinner." The men left and the pair cleaned up the dishes.

Lana spoke. "Curtis says I can move in here."

"What?" The gesture was surprising, but it didn't shock Christie that Curtis proposed the idea. It's not like he didn't have the room.

"I explained about finding a job which will leave the kids by themselves after school. They're eight and nine, and I know some people allow that, but I don't like the idea of them being by themselves. Not yet. I'm looking for work with an animal rescue or something like that in the area. I've always wanted to be a veterinarian but quit school when I got pregnant with Allie. And as you may know, you move a lot with the military, so it got further and further from happening. Curtis suggests I attend college instead of finding a job. I have the VA scholarship because of my husband, and I could stay here. That way, the kids would have someone around when they got off the bus." She looked up at Christie. "What do you think?"

"It's not what I think. It's what you think. Can you live with an older man you barely know? I like Curtis and all, but he's like my Pop—a handful."

Lana chuckled, "I'm sure he is. But he's like that puzzle piece. I can talk to him, and it's strange, but I can tell him everything, and he doesn't judge me. He'll sit there and say nothing and then bam, out of nowhere, he'll say something that makes it all seem so simple. I haven't said anything to the kids, but they'd love it. Especially Trey. He's always showing them things like how to tie a knot and plant seeds to grow corn, or whatever. He's like a living classroom for them. Plus, with us around, if anything were to happen, we'd be here to get help." She hung her head and rung her hands. "My kids won't get to know their father or their grandfather. I feel I owe them this. How many kids even have great-grandparents that they can spend time with?"

"When do you need to decide?" Christie sniffed as the reality of what Lana, Allie, and Trey had endured hit home. It would be a win-win for them both, and Christie would feel a lot better knowing someone was at hand if something happened to Curtis.

"Soon. If I leave the rental, I must give enough notice to the Websters. I do have to say, the idea of fulfilling my dream is exciting. The money I'm spending on rent would more than cover all the expenses I have now, so I wouldn't have to work. I received a life insurance settlement on Bobbie's death, and I've put it in savings. With my current support for the kids, I could attend college full-time."

"It sounds like a good plan. It's not like you'd live here forever."

Lana wiped imaginary crumbs off the table. "Curtis says if it doesn't work out, he can move into an apartment in the new barn." She cradled her head in her hands. "It's such a big step."

"Look, you don't need to figure it out tonight. Take some time and think it over. Listen, tomorrow's Saturday. How's about you let the kids hang out here with Curtis, and we go hit the shops in Comfort and Boerne and look around. I saw an owl statue in the Webster's office, and it's gone. I bet they sold it to a local antique shop. I'd want to see if I can find it as I really liked it."

"It's funny you say that. My dad said something one day about an owl. Like…" Lana cocked her head and looked right, pulling from memory. "Yep, that's it. He said the owl knew but said nothing."

"The owl knew, but said nothing? That's strange." A remembrance popped into Christie's mind. Kurt had said he'd wanted to tell Curtis something, but he'd never gotten the chance. Could the two items be related?

"Tomorrow then." Lana interrupted Christie's thought. "We'll be like the owl in the tree—on the hunt for our prey."

CHAPTER THREE

After waving goodbye to Curtis, Allie, and Trey, Lana offered to drive them into town, and Christie accepted. "You must excuse the mess, though. This is a true mom car!"

Christie laughed as she swiveled to see the books in the backseat along with martial art uniforms sticking out of a large, Army issue khaki-green duffle bag. Lana glanced over at Christie. "Sometimes, they each take hold of the handles and say that way they're holding where their dad's hand had held the bag, so they're holding his hand." Her face reddened, and she let out a low breath and looked out the driver's window.

"Listen, if you need to cry, you cry. Never let me stop you or make you feel you have to hide your feelings."

Lana wiped her tears and composed herself. "Thanks. So where to?"

"Let's hit the antique stores on Comfort's main street first."

After parking the car, they wandered from store to store, searching for the elusive owl to no avail. Driving into Boerne, they stopped at shops and were met with a lot of heads shaking no with their request. They were getting discouraged when someone said, "Wait a minute. I do remember that. I believe the store down the road bought the lot. As I recall, they didn't want to sell piecemeal but everything together, and that's hard for most shops who carry certain items."

After getting the name of the shop, they piled back into Lana's van. When they pulled up behind another vehicle at the stop light, Christie glanced out her window and could see that they were almost in front of Webster Realty. Two pristine white trucks were in the parking lot, and as they drove by, she spied Tyler and Emma in a heated argument. As they moved on past, Erik stood outside the front door. Their eyes connected for a split second, and a shiver ran down her spine at the intense animosity in his gaze.

She fought the urge to turn and look back at him. Now that he'd seen her with Lana, what would that cause him to do? For the first time in her life, Christie felt a fear she'd never experienced. Would Erik strike out at her or at Lana? What about Lana's kids? He had fought hard with Jess, who'd ended up black and blue from the attack. But Jess had jumped on Erik, and he was a tall teenager so closer in height and weight to a full-grown man. Surely, she was letting her imagination run away with her.

They neared the store and found a parking spot close to the entrance. Inside, Christie spied some of the furniture and accessories she'd remembered from the Webster's lobby. They looked around, and there, on a shelf by itself, sat the owl. Its eyes seemed to follow you as you walked toward it. Whoever had carved it had done an excellent job. The ear showed a crack, but it looked more like a line in the owl's ear, so it didn't detract from its unique appeal. Christie sucked in her breath at the price—a thousand dollars.

Lana came up to her. "Wow, the artist made it seem so life-like. It's beautiful. I can see how you would want it." She glanced at the price. "Yikes. They're awfully proud of it too."

Christie nodded and sighed. "Yep. Out of my budget. Oh well. I thought it might be a nice present for Pop. He's so hard to buy for, and I figured this would be something he would like."

"They might come down on the price. You could ask." Lana fiddled with a stack of old Life magazines on a nearby shelf.

The front doorbell rang, and Christie heard familiar voices. Emma's voice was pleading. "I'm sorry. I thought you'd like the new interiors. We can put it back the other way again."

Tyler growled, "I don't give a flying—" The door's bell rang again, muffling the expletives from him.

Lana and Christie made faces at one another but made no attempt to move. Better to stay hidden from view than to get caught up in the fray. An unfamiliar woman's voice joined Emma and Tyler. "Hello. I'm going to have to ask you to refrain from that language in here. If there's an issue…"

"There is an issue!" Tyler spat out at the woman. "My *wife* brought something here that wasn't hers to sell. I want it back. Now!"

The woman spoke quietly. "Sir, I'm going to have to ask you to remain calm."

Lana moved toward where she could see the group, and Christie joined her. They peered at the three people. Tyler appeared menacing, Emma chastised, and the woman trying to calm the situation firm. "What is it that you're talking about? I'd be happy to sell you the items back."

"It's mine. I shouldn't have to buy back what's mine!" He clenched and unclenched his fists.

"That may be true. But I have already paid for those items, and I must be reimbursed."

Tyler turned to Emma. "Give her the money back. Now!"

Emma flinched then turned to the woman. "I can use a card if that's what you accept." She started fishing in her purse for her wallet.

The woman replied, "I'll have to get a list of all the items and find—"

"I don't care about everything. Just the owl." Tyler twisted his neck and started searching the room.

Lana backed up, and a small vase tipped off a shelf and crashed to the floor. "Oh, c—"

The woman swiveled to them as they came around the shelving where they'd been standing. Emma's stunned expression revealed her shock at being overheard.

"We were looking back there and didn't want to interrupt." Lana pointed behind her. "We wanted to know if the price on the owl is negotiable."

The woman shook her head. "I did a lot of research, and that is a fair price for that quality of work."

"How much for the owl?" Tyler spun to face her.

"One thousand dollars." She replied in a matter-of fact response.

"Are you out of your—?" Another round of expletives followed.

"Sir! Again, I must ask you to stop or leave my shop."

Emma moved forward. "It was a mistake to have sold it. I didn't know it was a treasured family piece and will pay whatever you ask."

"No, I'm sorry."

"What do you mean?" Emma held her wallet. "I said I'd pay the full price."

"I mean I'm sorry, but I can't sell it you. Someone already bought it."

"You can't sell something that doesn't belong to you!" Tyler paced back and forth. "Who bought it? Give me their name. Now."

"I can't tell you that. It's against company policy."

He leant toward her. "I said. Give. Me. That. Name."

She stepped back. "I can't. It's sold. There's nothing I can do."

Emma placed her wallet back in her purse and pulled out a business card. "Please, if you could give my card to the buyer, I will pay double the price they paid. If you can work it out for me, I will give you a commission for your help." She handed the card to the woman, who hesitated to take it.

Tyler's back became rigid, and he stomped over to where Christie and Lana now stood. He pointed his finger in Christie's face. "Are you the buyer?"

"No. But if I was, I wouldn't sell it to you if you were the last person on earth." She shot back.

"I'm warning you—"

Lana moved closer to Christie. "You better leave now. Both of you."

Christie marveled at Lana's spine of steel, and knew she'd reveal how much dynamite she packed in her tiny frame.

Tyler turned on his heel and shoved the front door open but not before yelling to Emma, "You get that owl!" The bell on the door clattered.

After he'd left, the four women stood in an embarrassed silence while Emma regained her composure. Laughing, she said, "I'm sorry you had to see that. He's usually not like that. I didn't realize he'd had that statue in his family for generations or that it meant so much to him. Again, I apologize. Please, do let us know if the buyer will accept the offer. I'll pay whatever they request." She gave them a tight smile, adjusted her jacket, and left the shop.

"Well I never." The woman shook her head.

"I'm really sorry that happened to you. I'll pay for the broken vase." Lana pointed toward the pieces on the floor.

"Don't worry about it. Your help in defusing that situation is worth the little money I had in it." She shook her head. "What's the world coming to these days?" She went behind a counter and pulled a broom and dustpan from inside a small closet.

"Please, at least let me clean up the mess." Lana held out her hand, and the woman handed her the broom and pan.

They made their way to the back and all ended up looking at the large owl. The russet eyes seeming to stare at them. "Magnificent, isn't it?" The woman reached up and touched the base.

"The owl knew but said nothing." Christie said aloud. Why was Tyler so intent on this owl? She stared at it, but nothing obvious revealed itself.

After clearing the debris, Lana and Christie left the store. Lana was first to speak. "Was that crazy or what?"

"Yep. He's always been so calm and collected. I've never seen him like that. Though, it's been in a business setting when we've met." Christie shook her head. "I don't know about you, but I think I'm ready to call it a day." She heard a rattle behind her and saw the shop owner turn the sign to closed. She must have been as rattled by the encounter as they'd been.

The pair drove in silence back to Curtis's place, where they found the gate open. As they approached the house, Christie's stomach knotted. A silver Mercedes sat in front of the house. Erik.

They exited the vehicle, and Erik opened his car door. "I'm glad you're here. I know that we've been at odds, and I want to change that. Nick said we should push for the sale, and while I didn't want to, I went along with him. I figured that it would help out the old man…"

"It's getting really deep out here." Christie responded. She'd seen his face earlier. There hadn't been any change of heart.

"Fine. Believe what you want. But I want to make amends. Plus…" He took a step toward Lana and pointed between them. "Turns out we're family."

"I'm sorry, but I don't know you. From what I've heard, you've tried every way possible to get my great-granddad to give you land you don't deserve. No one does. It's his and his alone. If he wants to burn it to the ground, that's up to him."

"Maybe that's what he did with the barn." He cocked his head toward where the old barn had stood, now just a patch of scorched earth. "He's losing his marbles, you know."

"He is not." Christie fumed. "And if anyone started that fire, it was you. Just like you started our barn fire."

"Why can't you get it through your thick skull that I had nothing to do with that fire?" he retorted.

"Then what were you doing on our property? Plus, you said 'that fire,' which makes me believe you know about this fire."

He stammered. "Well, I … that's water under the bridge. I don't want to dwell on the past. I want us to start fresh. Get to know my niece."

"I'm not your niece, and I don't want to have anything to do with someone who's trying to rob Curtis." Lana crossed her arms.

"Listen. He's not getting younger. You live in a tiny, cramped space. You could be extremely wealthy if we worked together. That's all I'm saying."

Had Tyler or Emma shared where Lana lived? That Erik knew where Lana lived wasn't a welcome message.

Curtis came out on the front porch and stood listening.

Lana bucked up her back. "I'll have you know I don't have to worry about space, as I'm moving in here."

"What!" Erik swiveled to stare at Curtis, who simply grinned at the announcement. "You can't."

"I can, and I will." She crossed her arms.

Erik marched toward Christie. "This is all your doing. You're going to be sorry." He shook his fist at her.

"Get off my property." Curtis spoke at last. "You're no longer welcome here. Now, git."

Erik turned and gestured toward Curtis. "You had your chance, old man. What happens now is your own fault." He pointed to Christie. "And yours. You remember that."

Lana spoke before Christie could reply, "Remember this. You *ever* threaten my grandpa, my friend, or me again and it will be the last thing you do. Now like he said, 'Get off *his* property."

Erik left in a huff, the tires of his car sending up pieces of gravel and dust.

"Good riddance to bad rubbish." Curtis waited for the pair to join him on the porch. "Come on in. The littles are in the kitchen, coloring."

After deciding to have a light supper, Pop came over, and they ate egg salad sandwiches, with potato chips and dip. Curtis raved about Christie's pies, and after much cajoling from Curtis and Lana, she agreed to make a buttermilk pie for their next meal together. They ended the evening playing cards and swapping stories of their lives until late in the night.

Christie helped Lana carry the sleeping Allie and Trey out to the car and buckled them in before giving Lana a hug. "Thanks for deciding to try the situation with Curtis. I think it'll be good for him. Plus, now you've seen what we've been dealing with for so long. Erik's a bad penny that keeps showing up."

Lana hit the key fob to start the van. "I've felt like I was floundering for so long. My poor mother. She didn't know how to help, and as much as she loves the kids, they can be a handful in such a small place where they can't run and get any energy out. Now with Dad gone, I think she'll be happy knowing I feel good about where I'm heading. Plus, she's always encouraged me to pursue becoming a vet."

"That's great. Listen, we have quite a few horses over at our place right now. Could you, maybe, come over tomorrow or this weekend and just see if there's anything that may be a concern?"

"Happy to do that. Any chance of a ride?" She winked.

"I think we can manage that. Just let me know, and I'll make sure we're ready. I've been busy too, looking for different job opportunities. Nothing has appealed or seemed right. Pop says I need to take my time, but I feel pretty lazy not doing anything."

"I'm sure you're not being lazy. Your taking care of a bunch of horses is a lot of work." She smiled at Christie.

"Well, I should have gotten these two in their own beds hours ago." She glanced at her phone. "Geez, can you believe the time? After eleven." She stifled a yawn. "So much for those wild and crazy long nights of my youth. Now I'm ready for bed by ten most nights." The pair hugged again, and Christie waved her off. Pop had left for home earlier, and she let down the windows of the truck, still surprised by the humidity in the air no matter what the season.

At home, she brushed her teeth and was washing her face when a text pinged on her phone. She laid down the washcloth and wiped her hands on a towel. The text was from Lana.

Lana: You up? Call me.

Oh, no. Had something happened. She punched in her number. "Lana, are you okay? What's up?"

"Sorry. Didn't mean to scare you. I wanted to let you know I drove down Main Street on my way home. There were a bunch of police cars around the shop we visited earlier today. Someone smashed out the front window, and from the lights inside, looks like they tore up the shop."

"Oh, no!" Christie shifted the phone to her other ear. "Do you think Tyler did it?"

"It's strange timing; that's for sure. I stopped and asked what had happened. They didn't say much but appears to be teen vandalism. A few other shops in town were hit too."

Christie sighed. "Poor teens. They get a bad rap for things like that when a few cause problems for the many."

Lana agreed, then replied, "I do have to say: it seems fishy after what happened today. I wonder if they took the owl. Then, it would be game over for Tyler."

"I may see how the shop owner's doing tomorrow, as I have to run into town for some errands for Pop."

"Keep me posted."

"I will."

"Now, I have got to get some sleep before these two wake me up at six."

"Yikes." Christie and Lana said bye then rang off. Once in bed, Christie's mind refused to shut off.

Was it simply coincidence someone vandalized the shop the same day as the run-in with Tyler? Though, other shops had been hit too. One thing she knew for certain. There were two dangerous men in town who were both capable of destruction.

CHAPTER FOUR

The following morning, Christie drove into Boerne to grab ingredients for the buttermilk pie. First, though, she wanted to check to make sure the store owner was okay. Pulling up in front of the shop, she spotted a sheet of plywood over the window. The door to the shop stood open, and a large dumpster revealed destroyed shelving and large, broken pottery shards from ruined lamps.

Christie stepped through the door and gasped at the damage. "Hello?" she called out into the store.

The woman from yesterday came from around an armoire holding a bulky, large black trash bag. "Hi, sorry, we're closed."

"I'm not here to shop. Lana—the lady I was with yesterday—said she'd seen the police here last night. I wanted to stop by and see if you're all right."

"Just a minute." The woman walked past Christie and tossed the bag in the dumpster. She waved her hand. "Can you believe this mess? I can't understand why kids would do such a thing."

"Who said it was kids?"

The woman turned to Christie. "Do you know something I don't? The police said other shops got hit, and even a few cars had windows smashed in."

"Could someone be covering up breaking into your place?"

The woman wiped her hands on her jeans. "For what? As far as I can tell, everything's still here. Some just in pieces." She reached down and picked up a twisted picture frame and tossed it into a nearby bin. "Still, whether stolen or broken, my insurance rates will probably go through the roof now, but I can't recoup the loss without submitting a claim. Having your own business ain't for the faint-hearted sweetie; that's for dang sure."

"What about the owl?"

The woman sighed. "Really? I told you I sold the owl."

"No, I mean is it still here or was it taken?" Christie stepped back to avoid a pile of debris.

"Oh sorry. I'm a bit moody today. I apologize."

"No need. I can certainly understand." Christie waited.

Two men entered and spoke with the woman, who they addressed as Rose, about the window repair. When she returned to Christie, she said, "Listen, after that guy came in cussing me out, I took it to the buyer. I would have it delivered later, but I wanted it gone in case he or his wife came back." She sighed. "I hated to see that beautiful piece of art end up there, but,"—she shrugged—"you can't pick who gets what you sell."

"Do you have a book that lists all the deliveries and addresses, or do you keep that on your computer?"

"Nope. Old school. I use a book with a carbon copy so I can just rip out the page and give it to the delivery people." She motioned behind the counter. "I keep it back there."

"Can I see it, please?"

The woman shrugged. "Sure." She went behind the counter and pulled the tattered book from the shelf. "Here you go. What are you looking for?"

"If any pages are missing." She flipped through the book and handed it back to the owner, but not before seeing the address of the person who'd purchased the owl. "Looks like it's all here. Oh, well. I guess my hunch was wrong."

She surveyed the shop. "Listen, I have time to help out if you want me to pitch in."

"That would be great. Thanks."

After spending a few hours at the shop, Christie grabbed a few things from HEB and then drove home, where she took a nice hot shower. She called Lana and told her what she'd found out. It looked like random vandalism, nothing more.

"I'm going to check out the college today." Lana shared about her interview for school admission.

"I can pick up Allie and Trey if you don't know when you'll be back," Christie offered. "Or I can bring them out to Pop's."

"They're going directly to the after-school program through the martial arts school, so I'm all good, but thanks for the offer. Wish me luck!"

"No luck needed. I know they'll get a great student in you. Talk later." Christie signed off. She made her way out to the corrals and patted Champ on the muzzle. "Hey, boy. I'm looking forward to our ride soon. How about you?" The horse neighed as if in agreement.

Christie worked around the house and garden, but it wasn't long before curiosity about the person who'd purchased the owl invaded her thoughts. Finally, she grabbed her keys and put in the address she'd seen in the store book. It was an older part of Comfort where homes still had property that stretched around the house. As soon as Christie turned on the street, she knew exactly which house bought the owl. The yellowed limestone two-story house was one of the original homes built in the area. The yard and posts all held various owl sculptures or yard-art. Beyond the owls, terracotta pots full of assorted plastic flowers cluttered the entire front yard.

Christie crossed the cracked sidewalk littered with odds and ends. She rang the doorbell but heard no chime, so she knocked on the door. "Hello. Anyone home?"

No answer. A lacy curtain covered the glass door front. Christie listened and heard voices. She knocked again. Still no answer.

She heard a door slam against wood, so she left the porch and made her way over to the side of the house. Toward the back, a screen door closed and opened enough through momentum to create a rhythm effect. Christie glanced in the windows for any movement, but they were all covered with heavy lace drapes.

Grabbing the screen door, she saw the interior door stood open and revealed a small kitchen. The stench that wafted out toward her caused Christie to cover her nose. She pushed the door open. Inside, the sink was piled full with dirty dishes and food wrappers sat on every surface with other plates stacked on the table. Only a small path remained clear for walking. Christie had heard about hoarders, but this was the first time she'd experienced it. She listened and heard voices coming from the other room. "Hello! Anyone home?" She waited, but no reply came. Her nurse instincts took over, and she gingerly stepped into the room. "Hello. I'm coming in." Christie crossed to a hall entry. On either side, stacks of newspapers perched precariously in uneven columns. She inched her way down toward the voices, careful not to connect with any of the stacks, knowing one wrong move would send them all tumbling down.

What a fire hazard. Or a death trap.

She finally reached the room and saw a television playing a soap opera. In here, stacks of papers also surrounded the room. On one wall, an iron rack held an array of rolling pins. It was twisted, and some had escaped their holders and were lying around on the floor. Banker boxes formed one wall, and a recliner and tray table sat facing the television. Christie spied a pile of boxes, contents spilling everywhere, but there was no mistaking what shouldn't be there. An arm poked out from under a large box.

"Oh no." Bending down, Christie sought a pulse, but there was no life. She stood and took a deep breath to steady herself before calling 911.

The boxes, holding a multitude of owl statues and other animal figurines, must have collapsed on top of the person. She stepped back and looked around. A large, open box caught her eye. Before she even glanced inside, Christie knew it held the owl from the store. Styrofoam peanuts crunched underfoot as she made her way to peer into the box, expecting it to be empty. Instead, the owl sat inside. Maybe the woman had tried pulling the owl from the box, but it had been too heavy, and she'd collapsed into the stack of boxes behind her.

Wailing sirens snapped her from her thoughts. She stepped over another pile of papers to reach the front door. Opening the screen door, she waited until Sheriff Hugh Clauson approached.

"Hug." Christie pushed the door open. "Ugh, sorry, still old habit I'm trying to break."

"I'm used to it. Hard when you've had a nickname all your life people are used to calling ya. I don't have a problem with it. Just try not to use it in front of others." He sighed. "So what have we got here?"

Christie explained how she'd heard voices, and when no one responded, she'd investigated.

"Let's step outside. We'll be in the way while others are working, and there's no room." He surveyed the plastic flowers. "We've been out here before. Believe it or not, the yard looks pristine compared to what it looked like before. She used to have a couple of old broke down cars in the drive, grass overgrown up past your knees, and the back had so many piles, people were afraid if it caught fire, the whole street would go up. A nonprofit that works with the aging helped clean, but people with this mental illness can't bear to get rid of things."

"I hear you. I helped a friend clean out her mother's place. She had an old pressure cooker, but her daughter bought her an instant pot. She wouldn't let the daughter give it away. Her reason for keeping it was that she'd had it for fifty years. She didn't use it though."

"Yep, people are funny about their 'stuff.'" He took out a pad. "So, let's talk about the event."

"The boxes in the living room must have fallen on her. I checked for vitals but nothing."

"Stands to reason. Death trap just waiting to happen. They cleared that hall out, so these are all new stacks of papers." He shook his head. "Waste. She was a researcher on owls. She knew everything there was to know about them. But she ended up with that disease where you can't leave the house or something." He removed his Stetson and pushed back his hair before placing the hat back on his head. "We'll wait and see what the coroner says, but I think for now, you can probably go. I still have your phone number?"

Christie repeated it just in case he didn't have her newest number. She glanced back toward the porch where technicians were entering and exiting. "Okay, I think I'll go, then." She headed down toward her truck before turning back. "If it looks suspicious, if you're allowed, can you let me know?"

His eyes narrowed. "Is there a reason to think it's suspicious?"

"I'm not sure—"

"Tell me." He stuck his thumb in his gear belt.

Christie walked back over to where he stood and recounted the incident at the shop and the vandalism. "The only thing is… if he wanted the owl, he'd have taken it with him. So maybe I'm barking up the wrong tree."

"You know, ever since crime shows have come on in full force, everyone thinks they're a detective now." He huffed.

Christie retorted, "I don't watch those kinds of shows. Sorry I said anything."

"You wouldn't believe what we have to deal with on a daily basis. I'm not saying that your concerns aren't valid or have merit. But we've dealt with her before, and it looks like a sad accident. But tell you what, if I have anything that I can share with the public, I'll let you know." A suited technician came out and whispered something to him. "Gotta go." He tipped his hat, turning to listen to the man.

Christie pulled herself up in the truck's cab and cranked up the air conditioner. The fresh air cleared her mind and her sinuses. People were often cognizant of the elderly losing hearing or sight but losing the sense of smell was often another issue. She shook her head at how so many didn't have someone to care for them.

She called Lana before remembering she'd gone to San Antonio. She dropped that call and phoned Orchid. When she answered, Christie recounted the story to her. "Want to stop by for some tea?" Orchid inquired.

"Got anything stronger?" Christie grabbed a hairband from the console, and in one deft movement, stuck her curly auburn locks up into a messy bun. The cool hitting her neck felt great.

"Sarsaparilla?"

Christie laughed. "You know me too well. Be there in ten."

Driving down to Boerne, Christie decided what color she thought Orchid would have on her door. The eccentric older woman would often paint her front door wild, bright colors when it struck her fancy. But Christie didn't expect to see a door full of yellow happy faces when she pulled up at the curb.

She rang Orchid's doorbell. The spry woman answered the door wearing a multi-color caftan and matching turban. She wore long, dangling feather earrings. From the freckles that now dotted her brown skin, she'd spent some time outdoors lately.

Orchid reached up and gave Christie a hug. "I'm sorry to hear about your bad encounter."

"No. Thanks. I'm used to death after many years as a hospice nurse."

"No one should have to get used to death, but I'm sure you were a great comfort when they made their transition. However, there is a natural death, and there's what you've encountered." She motioned Christie inside.

The first time Christie had visited inside Orchid's home, the front room had been decorated in a mix of Victorian and contemporary. Now, it was sparse with minimal furniture, a fountain, and a wooden box containing sand that showcased intricately carved spirals and designs.

"First, the door and now, this. Orchid, you amaze me!" Christie waved at the room.

"I did the door because I knew Lana and the kids needed some cheering up. Hard not to smile when you see happy faces smiling at you when you leave the house in the morning and come home in the afternoon. They also glow in the dark." She winked. "Going to miss those two. Lana too. We have lots of fun. I made this sandbox, as it calms the mind of stress. The kids have used it almost every day, and Lana has taken a turn or two." Orchid looked up at Christie. "Want to give it a go? I'll get you a rake."

"Maybe later." Christie exhaled, suddenly exhausted after the adrenaline rush subsided.

"I got that sarsaparilla waiting for you. Even some ice cream if you want a float."

"Sarsaparilla alone is good." After taking a swig of the sweet soda, Christie exhaled deeply, "Ah, that hits the spot."

Orchid laughed. "Better?"

"Yes." Christie then shared about the encounter with Erik, about Tyler and Emma, the owl and the shop's vandalism, ending with finding the new owner of the owl dead.

"Wow. I have to agree with you. That's an awful lot of coincidences." She'd poured her soda into a glass and took a small sip before continuing. "The owl knew but said nothing. Let me ruminate on it a bit. Maybe while doing some raking. Sure you don't want to give it a go?"

"No, but thanks. I'm going to head home. I've got to make a buttermilk pie. You're more than welcome to come for dinner if you'd like."

"Thanks for the offer, but I've got my drumming class tonight."

Christie laughed. "Orchid, your social life and capacity for learning puts me to shame."

The woman joined in the laughter. "Honey, don't you fret. Once you get older, you realize that time's been a-wasting and you best get to doing all the things you've said you wanted to do when you were younger. Time waits for no human. So live life now while you can." She reached

over, and Christie expected her to hug her goodbye. Instead,

she laid a hand on her forehead and said, "Love is

surrounding you. Don't shut it out."

CHAPTER FIVE

As Christie drove home, she contemplated Orchid's words. She'd come home to Comfort and felt surrounded by love. Pop loved her, and she'd known his best friend, Curtis, since she was a child. He was like an uncle to her. She'd grown fond of Lana and her kids, and she felt they'd grown to care for her. So Orchid's statement left her curious. However, something kept niggling at her like a task you knew you needed to do but hadn't remembered. It lay just beyond reach.

"Ahh, well. I need to quit trying to remember so I can remember what it is!" Christie pulled her truck over under the large leafy oak to keep it in the shade. Stepping out of the vehicle, she heard chainsaws. After finally determining to build a cordwood house, they'd started clearing the property of the cedar trees, which would provide her home with great insulation and be fire retardant. A surveyor had been out, and they'd mapped out the house's location. Building it in the shape of an old grain tower had been a spurt of inspiration after Emma had tried to convince Christie to let them build her a McMansion.

Inside the house, she gathered the ingredients from the cold storage area and headed out to what they called the summer kitchen. She laughed. "As if there's any other season in Texas!" The state's summer heat stretched through most seasons.

She'd made the piecrusts a few days before, and they sat in the refrigerator. Christie gathered the ingredients for buttermilk pie. She'd received the recipe from Kris, a lady she'd met while visiting in Colorado. That trip to Carolan Springs with old college friends had been when her view of her life had shifted dramatically. The saying that you can't go back might be true, but it didn't mean you couldn't go forward wiser and better for your experiences.

Christie pulled organic lemons out of a paper bag. After washing them, she zested the lemons and then cut them open and, using a wooden tool, squeezed out the juice into a glass container. After juicing the lemons, she set them aside and cracked the eggs, breaking the yokes before she added the buttermilk. Once she'd done that, she added in the vanilla and butter, mixing all the ingredients together. She then added the dry ingredients of flour, sugar, and salt, folding them into the liquid mixture. Finally, Christie mixed it a bit more to ensure everything was incorporated and there were no lumps.

BUTTERMILK PIE RECIPE

Ingredients and Amounts

- Butter ½ cup, melted
- Buttermilk 1 cup
- Eggs 3 (beaten to break yolks)
- Vanilla 1 teaspoon
- Sugar 1 ½ cup
- Flour 3 tablespoons
- Salt (pinch)
- Pie Crust

Items Needed On Hand:

- Measuring Cups and Spoons
- Mixing bowls
- Wooden spoon with long handle or spatula
- Whisk

Instructions

Melt butter. In bowl break three farm-fresh eggs. Whip to combine. Add in buttermilk, butter, and vanilla. In another bowl combine the sugar, flour and salt until incorporated together. Add to the liquid mixture and stir to incorporate. With a spatula fold mixture into pie crust.

Heat oven to 375 degrees (190.55 C). Bake the pie for 10 minutes and then turn the oven down to 350 degrees (716.66) for 40 minutes. Check through oven window and if the crust is done/browning, cover with foil or a pie crust protector for duration of cooking time so the crust doesn't burn.

Cool before cutting. Best kept in refrigerator if any left over. Enjoy!

After doing it for the second pie, she put them into the oven and set the timer. As Christie cleaned the stainless steel counter, she whipped around and looked at the rack holding the metal rolling pin. Rolling pin. That's what had been bugging her. The rack of decorative and antique rolling pins had eight spaces. She'd spied five still in their holders, and two on the floor. That meant one was missing. She wiped off her hands and called Sheriff Clauson and explained about the rolling pins.

"She may have only had seven."

"I don't think so. Those were older. Probably before she started collecting the owls." Christie paced the room. "I think someone used it to kill her."

"Christie—"

"I know. I know. Too many crime shows. But something's not right. I mean the owl, then the shop vandalism, then—" A thought occurred to her. "Hug, please, give me the benefit of the doubt. Just see if you can check it out. Bye!"

"Hey there," Lana called out.

"Ack!" Christie turned to where Lana was standing outside the screen door. She laid her hand on her throat. "Sorry, you scared me."

"Okay to come in?"

"Yes, let me unlock the door. I keep it locked so it doesn't fly wide open and any bugs or leaves scoot in."

She walked over and hit the latch with her finger. Lana entered and looked around. "Wow, this is a pretty swell setup."

"Yep. My mother did a lot of cooking and baking, so Pop built her this outdoor kitchen. They screened the front portion for any bugs, and this part closes and locks with doors so everything, like the stove, fridge, and sink stay protected from the elements. We used it for canning parties when I was young."

"I can see why. That stove is massive."

"Yep, it took a lot of saving for my Pop to buy her that stove."

"Sounds like he really loved her."

"He did." Christie tried to remain composed. "We lost her when I was a teenager."

Lana came over and squeezed Christie's arm. "Oh, Christie, I'm so sorry. I can't imagine losing my mom."

"Well, I can't imagine losing a husband and now a father. We all lose people in our lives—some more tragically. Losing one person doesn't negate how others feel when they lose someone. We all grieve at some time in our lives."

Lana sang, "Circle of—"

Christie laughed loudly. "Thanks. I was getting a bit maudlin, wasn't I?"

"No. I like it. You often say such profound things. I think I should write them down for reflection later."

A snort escaped Christie. "Yep, that's me, the profound sayings person. These pies have some time left. Drink?"

Lana accepted a bottle of sparkling water, and they sat on the metal chairs in the corner. "So, tell me what you're thinking about this whole thing."

Christie recounted the discovery and also her idea about the rolling pin. "I'm wondering if someone came in, hit her on the head, and then knocked the boxes over to make it look like an accident."

"Possibly. There aren't any houses on the other side of the street?"

Christie nodded.

"You never know; someone could have seen something." She stared at Christie. "You think Tyler's involved, don't you?"

"I do. He was adamant about getting that owl. It just makes sense. Though, the owl was still at the house."

"Well, he couldn't have taken it. Someone definitely could have seen that, and he'd have had the finger of guilt pointed directly at him."

"The finger of guilt?" Christie grinned.

"Ha ha. Whateva." She waved her hand dismissively.

"No, I think you're right. He couldn't take the chance of being seen carrying that large box."

"We should go talk to the neighbors. See if they saw or heard anything."

"Why would they talk to us?"

Lana grinned. "Because we'll be investigators."

"But we're not investigators. That's a lie."

"Is it? We are investigating. Correct? As long as we don't say anything else, we're still telling the truth."

"Remind me to keep my eye on you." She pointed her finger at Lana, who laughed.

"Come on. You want justice for that woman, don't you?"

"Oh, no you don't. No heartstrings tugging, missy. But I am curious. Okay, I'm up for a bit of snooping but not cloak and dagger, okay?"

"Okay. No daggers, but I do have a killer velvet cloak." She winked as Christie groaned.

After she removed the pies from the oven, Christie covered them each with a screened cover. "You can never be too careful."

They decided they'd go speak to the neighbors tomorrow and would drive out in Lana's car, as it was gray, and Lana felt it would fit the profile better than Christie's red truck. Christie didn't have the heart to tell Lana most investigators didn't drive a mom van. She also asked Christie to wear something business-like and put her hair up in a bun. Christie shook her head in mock disgust but agreed to Lana's request.

That night, Curtis joined them, and they ate a simple dinner of beans, collards, and cornbread. Curtis had brought some venison sausage and fresh corn and tomatoes. While Lana sliced the tomatoes, Christie prepared the cornbread in an iron skillet and put it in the oven to bake.

Once the group had assembled around the old, scarred kitchen table, Christie announced that buttermilk pie was also on offer so to save room for dessert. Trey responded, "Buttermilk, no way. First these nasty green things—" he pointed at the collards.

"Those nasty green things have lots of vitamins in them and make you grow up strong. Do you want to be a strong man when you grow up?" Curtis pointed with his fork of collards.

The boy nodded and grimaced as he took a bite. "I still don't like these. But I want to be strong." He hurried to clear his plate. "Whew, done."

Christie replied, "I think you might like the buttermilk pie. Do you want to try some?"

He rubbed his belly. "A man can only try one new thing a day."

She stifled a chuckle. "Okay. Prudent. How about a hot fudge sundae if your mom says it's okay?"

Trey and Allie jumped up and danced around their mom. "Please, Mom. I know it's a school night, but we'll go to sleep. Promise and cross our hearts."

"Ugh. Fine. But just a small one." She pointed at Christie. "You're the devil."

"She's like the best auntie ever." Trey ran over and hugged Christie, who tousled the hair on his head. "Is it okay if I call you Aunt Christie?"

She smiled at him. "Sure. But you have to heed what my Pop says about calling."

Trey turned to Pop. "What's that?"

"You can call me by my name. You can call me by a claim, but whatever you do, don't call me late for supper!" Pop responded.

Trey clutched his belly and giggled. "That's funny." He ran back to Christie. "When can we have the sundaes?"

Christie grabbed the ice cream while Lana cut up a banana. She heated the fudge sauce and drizzled it over the ice cream. Christie said, "Whipped cream? Sprinkles? Cherry on top?"

Trey and Allie's head bobbed up and down in assent. Lana settled the kids with their sundaes and books.

She pointed at the pair. "Why do I feel you bought all that to have on hand for them?"

"No idea what'cher talking about." Pop grinned.

"Sure." Lana went behind Pop and hugged his neck. "You two will be the death of me."

"Speaking of deaths, did I hear right that you found someone dead today, Christie?" Curtis pushed a toothpick to the side of his mouth and waited.

"No point in denying it. Yes, I found a woman who died. Stacked boxes fell on her."

Pop spoke. "But I can see as clear as day that you're having none of that. What ya thinking?"

Christie lowered her voice so the kids wouldn't hear and explained about the owl, the shop destruction, and then the lady's death.

"Hmmm. That does bear some pondering." Curtis stroked his cheeks, the sound of his grizzled beard sounding like sandpaper. "Let me ponder on that a minute." He chewed on the toothpick, lost in thought.

Christie shared about them going to see if any neighbors remember anything.

Curtis banged his fist on the table. "That's it!"

Everyone jumped at the sound, and the kids ran in from the front room, their eyes big as saucers. Lana escorted them back to the living room to watch a documentary.

Once she'd returned to the kitchen, Curtis spoke. "Sorry 'bout that. I will try better to remember 'bout them littles in the future. Now, let's think about this.

"If you dun kilt someone and you needed to hide a weapon, where would be the best place to hide it?"

The group shrugged. "Okay, let me put it like this. If I had a gun I wanted to hide, where would be the best place?"

Pop nodded. "Exactly."

"What are you two talking about?" Christie threw her hands into the air. "You're not making any sense."

Curtis leant over the table toward her and Lana and whispered, "What if someone wasn't breaking in to steal something? What if they broke in to put something there?" He sat back, satisfied.

"Oh, my gosh." Christie rose and paced the kitchen. "You're right. You'd need to take it in case of DNA transfer, but you'd also need to get rid of it. You couldn't take the chance of someone finding it and then saying anything about where they'd found it. The easiest way would be to let someone else contaminate it with their DNA and get rid of it." She yelped. "The dumpster. If the rolling pin got thrown there, we may never find it."

She grabbed her phone and called. "Sheriff, please bear with me. I think someone murdered that lady, and they did it with a rolling pin. Then they threw it through the broken window of the antique store." She waited.

Finally, Sheriff Clauson spoke. "You may be on to something there. Turns out, the head wound doesn't correlate with the boxes. It may have been used to knock her out and then push the boxes on top of her. I'll get deputies over to the store to secure that dumpster. Thanks for your help. And I do mean that." He rang off.

Christie sat down. "How about that? Sounds like he's actually taking me seriously now."

"Now don't you go carrying on, miss sassy satisfied pants." Pop tipped his chair up, causing Christie to cringe at the thought of him falling and re-injuring his shoulder. "Here's the thing. You almost done got yourself killed, sticking your nose in, and now ya done got Lana involved." He crooked his neck toward the living room, where the kids sat engrossed in the animal show. "You want to cause trouble for them young'uns? Stop this right now. No more snooping. You either." He pointed his gnarled finger at Lana.

Lana and Christie glanced at one another. "We promise we won't go anywhere near that shop," Lana replied.

CHAPTER SIX

Christie pulled out the only suit that she had in her wardrobe. It was a dark navy trouser suit she wore to patient's funerals. She'd kept it in the back of the closet, but never expected to wear it again. Even in the air conditioning of her room, she could feel the sweat beading up on her brow. She took off the jacket and slung it over the chair while she worked her hair up into a French twist.

"You ready?" She heard Lana call out from the front room. Christie glanced at the clock. Time to get a move on.

"Yes, coming." She grabbed the jacket and opened the door. Lana wore a black suit with a round metal pin on her lapel. She also wore dark aviator glasses. She handed a pair to Christie. "Here, wear these."

"I thought we're investigators, not spies or the secret service."

Lana shrugged. "This way, they can't see our eyes. And no offense but let me do the talking."

"You do know I'm older than you, and I have some experience?" Christie draped the jacket over her arm.

"Yep, but I'm not known as much here. If you talk, they could recognize you."

Christie sighed. "I guess you do have a point there." She pushed the dark glasses onto her head. "Lead on, oh wise one." She shrugged into the jacket.

Instead of coming into the neighborhood from the standard direction, Lana drove in another way, which gave them a view of most of the street. No cars or deputies cruisers sat in front of the house, and the street looked quiet. Lana turned to Christie. "Okay, I pulled a picture with Tyler on it, and I'll show that to them. Let's see what we get."

Driving toward the neighbor's house, Lana parked a few doors down on the block. They made their way to the next-door neighbor. Lana rang the bell. She knocked on the door while Christie stood behind her. She knocked again, and finally an elderly lady answered the door. She was bent over and held on to a walker. "Hello." She looked up at them with eyes clouded by cataracts.

"Hello, Ma'am. We're investigating your neighbor's tragic accident." Lana flipped open some credential wallet, which she quickly put back in her pocket.

"Speak up, dearie." The woman cupped her hand to her ear.

Christie moved forward, knowing she would hear her loud voice better than Lana's soft one. "We want to ask you some questions about your neighbor. If you saw anything or anybody—"

Lana pulled a picture from her pocket and held it up. "Ma'am did you see this man next door this week?"

The woman squinted at the picture. "I need my glasses. Come in." She pushed on the hook holding the screen door and started walking back to the living room. Sitting down in an old stuffed chenille chair, she picked up the eyeglasses on the adjacent table. Lana handed her the picture. The woman squinted at the photo before grabbing a magnifying glass held upright in a mason jar. She moved the glass up and down. Lana reached over and touched the photo which showed Nick, Erik, Tyler, and Emma from an older article about their joint business enterprise partnership. "Yep, he was here." She handed the photo back to Lana.

Lana pointed to Tyler. "This man was here a few days ago?"

The woman used the magnifying glass to look to where Lana pointed. "No, not him." She pointed with a knobby, arthritic finger. "Him." The woman had pointed to Erik Stewart. Lana and Christie exchanged glances. The woman looked closer at the photo. "I don't remember when, but she was here too." She handed the photo to Lana.

After politely refusing a cup of coffee, the pair walked back to the car. "What do you think?" Christie flung her coat in the back seat and loosened her collar, sweat already collecting on her back.

"Maybe she's mistaken. She can barely see or hear. Maybe she got it wrong. What would Erik be doing over here?" Lana swung toward the open field and pointed, "Unless, he's trying to get property over there."

Christie sighed. "What about Emma? Do you think she found out who'd purchased the owl and tried to buy it back?"

"Are you insinuating Emma killed that woman?"

"No. Ugh. I don't think this even helps us. Just adds more questions and no new answers." She spied another house past the woman's they'd questioned. "Give me that picture. I'm going to go ask the other neighbor."

"Want me to come?" Lana had pushed the glasses up on her head, and wisps of hair escaped from the tight bun.

"No. I'll do it. Back in a minute."

Christie left, and when she returned, she held a business card in her hand. "Look. Erik's card. Supposedly, he's going around, getting feedback on adding in a large box store at the edge of town. That must be the project they were working on with Webster Realty."

Lana turned to Christie. "Do you think Erik went to that woman's house to get the owl for Tyler? Maybe he killed that woman."

"While I wouldn't put it past him doing anything, I just can't see it, though. What would be his motive? I guess Tyler could have asked him to contact the woman on his behalf about the owl. But here's the kicker. She also saw Emma, but not sure what day. I just don't get it." Christie reached over and cranked up the air conditioning to full blast. "Tyler just doesn't seem the sentimental type. I mean the owl is a beautiful work of art but—"

"That reminds me. What happens to all her things— including the owl?"

"I would think it would go to her estate. I wonder if she has any family." Christie eyed the property, the plastic flowerpots laying haphazard on the lawn now.

"We need to do a stakeout." Lana faced Christie.

"What? Are you out of your mind? I don't have time to sit around seeing 'what'?"

"I dunno. Okay, what's your idea?"

Christie pulled her bag from the floorboard and dug her phone out of the bottom. "Sheriff Clauson, please. Yes, I'll hold." Lana spoke when Christie put a finger to her lips. "Sheriff, a quick question for you. Did the deceased have family? I'd like to purchase an owl statue she has." Christie listened. "Um, hm. Oh, is that right? Okay, thanks." She ended the call.

"Well?" Lana fidgeted with a ring on her finger.

"You will never believe this. She had no relatives other than a brother in Minnesota who's in a nursing home. They sold the entire contents to Rose."

"Wait. So Rose sold her the owl, and now she owns it again so she can sell it again? What if Rose changed her mind and told Emma?"

Each lost in her own thoughts, Lana drove Christie home. The pair agreed to meet up to go horseback riding early the next morning. Lana would stop by Rose's shop and find out about the owl and if she'd spoken to Emma. She'd let Christie know if she found out anything else about Erik's possible involvement.

The next day, Lana arrived after dropping the kids at school, so they could ride before it grew miserably hot. Together, they worked on the horses, brushing and preparing for saddling. After donning large-brim hats, the pair set off on their ride. A breeze would occasionally cool them off as they made their way past the build location of Christie's home.

"I can see why you chose this area. I guess the cut of the land and being up a bit higher allows for that breeze. It's nice. Plus, what a great view." Lana twisted her back, resting her hand on the saddle. "Yep, really nice. I have to say, I'm going to enjoy having lots of space around without neighbors next door. Except for Orchid. The kids and I'll miss her, but I've promised we'd visit and have invited her out to the house too."

They set the horses to a trot, and Christie showed Lana where Curtis had almost died. "See that spot? That's where somebody dug the hole, right in front of where that new post is now. I think someone hid it, so Curtis never saw it. Then, when he fell, he hit his head on the cairn that were placed there." She pointed to where the rocks had stood.

They made a pass around the property and returned to the barn where Lana and Christie cleaned the horses and led them to the paddock.

"Champ, you're a great horse. Thanks for the ride." Lana stroked his muzzle while Lana led the other gelding into the adjoining paddock.

"I've got time if you want help to muck out the stalls." Lana wiped her forehead and stuck her hat back on.

"Are you kidding me? Who'd ever refuse help mucking?" The pair grabbed pitchforks and set to work. After they finished, they laid down new straw.

"I can see that this is probably Champ's stall, and is this one of your mares?" Lana pointed to the stall.

"Yes, how d'you know that?" Christie inquired.

"Males tend to go in the middle of the stalls and females on the sides. Not always, but often." She went into the mare's stall and, with her gloved hand, picked up some of the manure. "Hmmm, this doesn't look right." Christie joined her. "I agree, but what do you think it is?"

"Not sure. Have a bag I can put this in to show my professor? Let's take a look at her." The pair walked over to the mare, and Lana looked her over. "Her belly seems a bit distended. She hasn't gotten any moldy hay by any chance?"

"I don't think so. But I'll check it all now that you've said that. The last thing we need are horses getting colic or worse."

After taking off their gloves, they washed their hands in the barn's sink. The pair moved to the shady backside, where they sat on chairs and sipped iced tea from the cooler Christie had brought to the barn.

Lana spoke. "I didn't have time to speak with Rose yet. Do you want to go speak with her?"

"Not until after a shower. Want to meet for lunch?" Christie crossed her booted ankles and set them on the arm of another chair.

"Okay. I'll head home, grab a shower, and we can meet there." Lana rose and stretched her back before removing her boots and grabbing a pair of flip-flops she'd brought from the car. "Let me grab the poop and go."

"Now, that's not something you hear every day." Christie chuckled.

CHAPTER SEVEN

The shower eased the tension in Christie's muscles, and she allowed the water to beat on her neck. After emerging from the shower, she wiped the mirror with her hand and used a pick to untangle her curly russet locks. She knew there was no point in trying to dry it as it always grew into a huge, frizzy nest. Dressed, she called to see if Lana was ready to meet up. As Christie had been thinking about it, she really liked the rack with all the antique rolling pins and wanted to see how much Rose would price it for selling. She already envisioned it in her new kitchen over a designated area with a marble top that would be useful for baking pies and bread.

Christie drove down the highway, exiting Bandera Road before a quick turn onto Main Street, then veering onto 46 to meet Lana at The Dodging Duck. After they'd ordered their meals, Christie asked, "So, when are you planning to move out to Curtis's place?"

"Well, I've got some time. He told me to do whatever I wanted to feel at home there, so I'm going to paint the master bedroom and the kids' rooms to start."

"Are you hiring someone to do the painting for you?" Christie squeezed a lemon into her water.

"No. I can do that. I'll probably start this weekend. I need to get a move-on, as I received acceptance from the college. Looks like I'll be a student come the fall." She shook her head. "I have to pinch myself sometimes. Moving here seemed like the worst thing but has turned out to be one of the best things to happen to me in a while." She shrugged. "Like Dad used to say, coincidence is God's way of remaining anonymous. I know he'd be pleased as punch that I'm finally pursuing my dream."

"I still can't figure what he meant by what he said, though. 'The owl knew but said nothing.' What do you think he meant?"

"No clue. My dad would often say things like that aloud, but he wasn't speaking to any of us. Instead, it was something he was saying to himself."

The waitress interrupted their conversation as she set plates down in front of them. "This looks yummy. Glad we grabbed lunch out, or I'd probably be eating leftovers."

Lana stabbed a forkful of salad before pointing toward Christie. "This is the way I see it. Dad was working at Webster Realty. Maybe he saw or overheard something he shouldn't have. I guess he was trying to work it out in his head." She halted.

Christie could see the struggle on Lana's face and the memory of her father's murder still fresh. "I'm sorry, Lana.

If you don't want to talk, or we can certainly change the subject, which isn't a great one for lunch."

"That's the problem. I have to. Even if it hurts to my very core. My dad deserves justice." She took a bite of food and chewed.

"Okay. I agree. I'll help any way I can." She set her fork down. "Here's what we know for sure. Your dad found out something at the Webster's. He had told Curtis he knew something, but he didn't tell Curtis what it was. He met Curtis late at night to tell him that he was his son. Someone killed him. Those are indisputable facts. Are we agreed on those?"

"Yes. Sounds right." Lana wiped her mouth and took a sip of the lemonade.

"So, that leaves us with a ton of questions. First, what did your dad find out? Was it worth killing him to keep secret? Who discovered he knew the secret, and most importantly, what was the secret? Or did Nick kill your dad because he was your father's son and, thus, his true heir? Finally, what does that stupid owl have to do with all of this?" Christie tapped her fingers on the table.

"Agreed. Lots of dead-ends." Lana pointed at Christie's plate. "You've barely eaten anything. I thought you were hungry?"

"I am, but it upsets my stomach. I'll take this to go." Christie motioned to the waitress for a box.

"Do you need to go home, or are you still up for—?" Lana stopped as Christie's phone rang.

Christie pulled it from her bag and answered, "Hello. Yes, of course. We'll be over in a bit."

After she ended the call, Lana spoke. "You should see the look on your face. Who was that?"

"It was Rose. She wants to know if I still want the owl. She's willing to sell it to me for five hundred dollars."

"What!" Lana slapped the table with her hand. "What about Tyler and paying whatever price she wanted?"

"I don't know. We need to get over there and find out. For someone to be so adamant about something and then turn around and say they're not interested, we have to figure this out."

Lana treated Christie to lunch, and they agreed to meet at Rose's shop. They parked and strolled down to the store. Rose had replaced the broken window with a shiny new one showcasing a display of various Texas signage.

They entered the door, and no bell sounded. Christie looked up at where the hanging bell used to be located. They had removed it. Instead, a mounted camera stood in its place. Rose was at the front corner, sitting on a stool and writing in a book. She looked up and waved. "Just a minute. New computer."

"No worries. Take your time. We'll wander around." Lana moved off to look at some dishware while Christie ambled through the aisles. On a shelf in the corner stood the owl.

Rose joined her. "As much as I love that piece, I'll have more than made my money off it and ready to see the end of its tail-feathers. So, five hundred dollars and it's yours. Trust me, that's a steal."

"What about Tyler Webster? I thought he wanted it and would pay anything for it."

A strange look crossed Rose's face. "That man is a nutcase. I called him up, and he said he no longer wanted it. He wouldn't pay a dime for it." She shrugged. "You never know with people like him. Sometimes, I think they just want things because they don't have them or to show how powerful they are." She sighed. "So what'll it be? Want it or not? I figured I'd give you first dibs since you helped me clean up the shop."

"Yes, I want it." Christie looked around. "Do you have the rack and the antique rolling pins out yet?"

Rose cocked her head and glanced at Christie. "How do you know about that?"

"The sheriff told me that you'd bought up the house contents, and I saw it at her house."

"You were there?"

Christie nodded. "Yes, I'm the one who found her."

"That gives me the shivers." She motioned to the back. "There are still lots of things packed. You wouldn't believe how much stuff we had to determine if it was trash or worth saving—oh wait, I guess you would, since you saw that house. The only saving grace was that it was a smaller home. She couldn't manage the stairs any longer, so upstairs wasn't like that downstairs mess. Thank goodness."

They walked to the front counter, and she scrolled down the list in the book. "Let's see. Yep, the rolling pin rack is still boxed up. I'm missing one of the rolling pins. But one person who helped thought we had one that would fit right in."

"Where? Can I see it?" Christie replied.

"It's not here. It had some damage. We think it broke when all the vandalism happened. So it's at the carpenter shop."

"Oh, no." Christie tilted her head back, a deep sigh escaping.

Rose glanced up at Christie. "What? So you don't want that one?"

"It's not that. I think that the pin may have been used to kill her."

"What do you mean?" Rose pulled her phone from under the counter.

"It's just a hunch. But if they clean it or fix it, they could destroy vital evidence."

Rose punched in the numbers and waited. Finally she spoke into the microphone. "Don't touch that rolling pin yet. I want to look at it first. Please keep it in the bag containing it." She ended the call. "There. Hopefully, it hasn't been touched yet. What else do we need to do?"

"Call the sheriff and let him know about it. They need to check it out and eliminate it if it turns out to be nothing."

"Okay." She took the number from Christie. "Anything else?"

"I'll definitely take that owl and, if the rolling pin rack is manageable, that as well."

"Two hundred?" Rose inquired.

"How about one fifty?" Christie countered.

"Okay. That works. I'll write it up after I get off the phone." She punched in the numbers and while she was talking, Christie made her way over to Lana who'd been looking in the store.

"So what are you thinking?"

"I found a lot of neat things, but I shouldn't buy anything until we actually get moved in and see what we have and what we still need. A lot of items are in storage, so I need to go through all that stuff too."

"Good idea. I can help you with the house later."

"That would be great. Trey's all excited, as Curtis will let him ride up on the tractor with him."

Friday afternoon arrived, and Christie met Lana out at the Altgelt Ranch. The kids were out playing on the tire swing, with Curtis and Pop sitting nearby. Lana waved Christie into the house. "Come and see this room. It's unbelievable."

Lana led Christie down the hall to a room with large double doors. Christie stepped back while Lana opened them. Inside, an air of disuse permeated the room. Patio doors looked out toward the backyard, and a wood fireplace took up the main corner. A king-size bed took up much of the space, but the room also held bookcases and an antique dresser from the forties or fifties. Lana grabbed Christie's wrist and pulled her into the room. "Look here." She pointed toward the opposite end of the chamber.

When Christie looked through the door, she found a good-size bathroom, complete with a clawfoot tub. A corner shower appeared to be a later addition. From there, his and her closets completed the space.

"Wow. I didn't realize this room was the entire width of the house. It's like a huge suite of rooms. Lots of light, and that patio door is really nice."

"Yes, I've already envisioned a nice little table and chairs out there where I can study at night. Curtis says he'll enclose the area with a roof and screen in the sides so it will keep out pesky mosquitoes. There's almost more space in this one room than I have in my entire house. I love that fireplace area with the bookcases. I can sit there and read to the kids or simply chill out at night."

"Lovely. What about the kids' rooms?" Christie asked.

Lana walked out into the hall before opening a door on the left. "This one will be Allie's. The one across the hall is Trey's. They're the closest ones to the master, so I'll be near for them. For now, we're going to use the other two for storage, but Curtis said it would be pretty easy to convert one of them to another bathroom if needed."

The pair set to work cleaning, dusting, and packing things in boxes. They cranked up the music and were dancing around the room when a male voice interrupted them. "I heard you all could use some muscle to move furniture."

Lana squealed, and Christie blushed at being caught out dancing wildly around the room.

Mike laughed. "Don't worry about me." He rolled up his shirtsleeve, displaying a tattoo of the Gadsden flag. "Jess!" He yelled over his shoulder, "Hurry with that snack."

Christie set down the dust cloth. "You obviously haven't seen him inhale his food. I don't know where he puts it all. He eats and eats and doesn't gain an ounce. Not fair when I eat anything, and it goes straight to fat."

"I think you look just fine," Mike replied as Jess came into the room, munching on a sandwich. "I thought you just ate cereal."

"I did, but I was still hungry." He took another big bite.

"Okay, well, finish that up and wipe your hands so we can get started." Mike nodded toward the bed. "Are we keeping that or taking it apart?"

Lana chimed in. "Apart. If I keep it, I may either paint or re-stain it. For now, we need everything out of here so we can paint."

"Okay, let me get my tools out of the truck." He yelled out, "Jess!"

"Yes, sir?"

"Go grab my tool bag and bring it in here." He went over to the bed and began inspecting it. "Where are you moving this bed?"

Lana piped up. "Let me show you."

Mike followed her down the hall to the extra bedroom. When Mike returned, he studied the bed and asked, "What else is going in there?"

Christie could see the wheels turning in his mind. He must be an analytical thinker. Maybe he could help her, and Lana puzzle out some of the unanswered questions about the owl, the dead woman, and if it had any connection to Lana's father's death.

While Mike and Jess worked on moving furniture, Christie and Lana finished the boxes. "I'm calling it quits for the day."

Curtis stood in the doorway. "Sounds right. Now, you guys, come grab some grub. Me and R.C. rounded up some vittles." Curtis motioned to the group to follow him to the kitchen.

"I'm starving," Jess said and hurried after Curtis.

"Geez. That kid has a hollow leg." Mike waited for Lana and Christie to go down the hall.

In the kitchen, Curtis and Pop had grilled hamburgers and hotdogs along with chips and sodas.

Trey and Allie opted for hotdogs and begged to go out on the swing to eat them. Jess joined them, no doubt to be away from the adults. At the table, Pop said, "Mike, I thought you weren't coming in until tomorrow."

"I figured I could drive in tonight, so might as well." He took a bite of his hamburger and swiped a chip in some ranch dip.

"You kids. All work and no play. You need to get out. Go dancing." Curtis motioned to them.

"I'm tired." Christie chimed in.

"Ahh, come on. It'll be fun. I haven't been dancing in forever. What do you say, Mike?" Lana nudged his arm.

"I'm game. What about it, Christie?"

"You two go." She cut her hamburger in half.

Pop spoke up. "No. You go too. You never do anything fun."

"I do."

"When?"

"Pop, it's late, and I'm tired."

"Late? In my day, we got up before dawn, milked the cows, worked the fields, and danced with pretty girls all night."

"Argh. Okay. Okay. Next I'll be hearing how you walked miles to school in the snow."

"And it was uphill both ways." Lana and Mike chimed in together.

Mike spoke. "Well, since that's settled, I need to go get cleaned up before Jess hogs the space." While Mike worked the oilfield, Jess had been living in a small trailer next to Pop's house. Mike often stayed with Curtis when he came into town, but with the room getting filled with boxes, he would have to make different plans soon.

"Nah, you can still use the bathroom here, and the bed's still usable for tonight." Curtis waved the girls off. "I'll watch the littles, and you go and have fun. Now scoot."

Lana crossed over and kissed Curtis on the cheek. She then told the kids they'd be spending the evening with

Curtis and Pop. Allie and Trey's excited voices carried into the kitchen.

"Pick you up in forty?" Mike asked Christie, who simply nodded her head.

CHAPTER EIGHT

Christie didn't understand why she felt butterflies in her stomach. Three friends were going out dancing. That was all. She dressed in a new turquoise slip dress that coordinated with her boots. She grinned at the row of boots lined up against the wall. Work boots, riding boots, day-to-day boots, going-out boots. And next to them, flip-flops. She'd definitely gone back to her Texan roots.

Knowing the dancehall would probably be hot and crowded, she fixed her hair in a half-up, half-down style. This kept her unruly curls off her face, yet still free in the back. She heard a loud masculine clearing of the throat from the living room. "Hello?"

"Almost ready." She called out. Grabbing a tube of lip stain, she applied it before dropping it in a fringed suede bag. Christie walked out to the front room, and Mike stood up from the couch, smiling.

"Worth the wait. You look lovely." He crooked his arm, making Christie's butterflies jump. "Ready?"

"Yes. Thanks." She ignored his arm and fiddled in her purse for her keys. "I'll drive."

"If that's what you prefer." He waved his hand toward the door.

They drove down to Boerne in silence, and Lana bounded out to the truck. "I'm glad you're here. Beyond ready to have some fun for a change." She hopped up in the back seat.

Mike turned around and smiled at her. "You look very nice this evening."

See, he was just being polite. Quit acting like a teenager. What's the matter with you?

On the drive, Lana shared with Mike all that had been happening. He let out a low whistle. "Whoa, I don't like the sound of that. You two aren't doing anything foolish, are you?"

Lana crossed her arms. "No, of course not. But if I find out what happened to this woman, it may help me discover the truth about my father."

"Leave it to the sheriff's office. They know what they're doing."

Christie put on her blinker and merged into the other lane. "True, but we can find out things they may not think about."

He put his hands up. "Just saying. Curiosity. Cat."

"We're careful."

"Good to hear." He adjusted his seatbelt so he could face toward Christie. "What's up with this Erik guy? Curtis tells me he won't stop pestering him about selling the property. And did I hear right that he attacked you? He better not come 'round me. No man should lay a finger on a woman."

"Or vice versa." Lana chimed in.

"Yep. So what's the story?"

Christie filled him in on Erik's partnership with Tyler and how they were scheming to purchase a portion of Curtis's land along with some of their property and then develop an area with multi-million dollar homes.

"That sounds horrible. Why would you spend so much money on a house that you can pretty much reach out and touch your neighbor's house?"

"Agree. But they don't care about who actually lives there; they're just after lining their pockets."

They arrived to find the parking lot full of lots of trucks. Guys in crisp shirts, pressed jeans and cowboy hats stood around outside talking while groups of young women flirted with them on their way inside. Suddenly, Christie felt ancient. The last time she'd been out dancing like this, she'd been in her twenties. Now in her later forties, she felt outdated and unattractive compared to what she was seeing.

Lana fit in with that crowd and practically bounced with excitement as they made their way across the parking lot. Mike reached out and touched Christie's hand, which made her gasp. He leaned in and whispered, "I don't know about you, but I feel like the old man here. Thankful you came, as I can see that those guys think I'm a lucky man."

What? Had he read her thoughts? What did he mean about the guys?

She turned to see a couple guys next to the tail bed of a truck. One smiled and tipped his hat at her. Feeling like a deer caught in the headlights, she hurried to join Lana.

Lana took Christie's arm in hers. "This is going to be so much fun." Mike treated them, and they received a hand stamp. Inside, the music blared as couples two-stepped on the floor.

"Ready to go?" Mike offered his hand to Christie.

"Um, maybe you and Lana should dance first."

Mike laughed. "No need to worry about Lana." He tipped his head toward the dance floor, where Lana and a young man were already moving away. He held out his hand. "Unless you'd like to get something to drink first."

"No… I haven't danced in a long time, so…"

"Don't worry; it'll come back to you." He lightly touched the small of her back and led her onto the dance floor. In a minute, it was like they had danced together for years. They easily moved in sync with the music, and as she grew more comfortable, she relaxed and grinned broadly.

"This is so much fun."

"Good." He spun her easily, and they two-stepped around the floor. The night passed quickly, and the trio chatted during dances. Finally, they agreed to leave after one more line dance.

"I can't believe I've stayed out after midnight. The last time I did that, I was in high school." Christie pulled her bag from off her shoulder to grab the keys. "Thanks for forcing me to get out of the house. This did me good."

"Me too. Definitely better going out with you lovely ladies than being stuck with a houseful of smelly old men," Mike guffawed.

The drive home was uneventful, but as Christie turned onto Lana's street, a fire truck and other response units stopped them. Christie pulled over into the first spot, and Lana jumped out of the back cab and raced toward the gathered crowd. Mike and Christie quickly caught up to her and gasped as they saw Lana's home engulfed in flames.

"Oh, Lana. I'm so sorry." Christie tried to grab hold of Lana, who marched toward a policeman.

"Ma'am, you can't be here." He held up a hand to stop her from going forward.

Lana raised herself up and pointed. "That's my house!"

The policeman nodded and escorted her off to speak with other officers.

"Shoot. Looks like we'll have to wait to find out what happened. I wonder—" She turned toward Orchid's house, where the woman was signaling to Christie from her porch.

"Come on." Mike followed behind her until they met Orchid at the stoop.

Orchid wore a bright multi-colored turban on her head, a muumuu style robe, and her face shone in the fire's light across the street. "Sad, sad thing." She took in a deep breath. "Was that Lana I saw?"

"Yes, we went out for the night. This is Mike." She gestured toward him. "This is Orchid Merryweather."

Mike tipped his hat. "Nice to meet you, Ms. Merryweather."

"You too." She pulled her hand from her pocket, wiping her nose with a tissue. "What about Allie and Trey?"

"They're out at Curtis's. We stopped by so Lana could pick up her car."

"What a relief. When I heard the fire trucks and saw the home ablaze, my heart broke, thinking any of them were at home."

"I can imagine. Thankfully, they were away and safe." Mike responded.

Christie crossed her arms, "Convenient, too." She spied Lana in the crowd looking for them. "Lana, over here!" She waved with both arms.

Lana joined the trio. "Well, I've been saying I wanted new furniture. I guess now it will be less to move."

"Still, your memories and—"

Lana tilted her head toward her minivan. "Not to worry there. I'd already boxed up much of that small stuff and put it in the van to take over to Curtis's tomorrow. Much of our main stuff is in storage still, so between me, Trey, and Allie, we may have six to eight boxes between us."

"That's good to hear," Mike interjected. "What did they say?"

"They wouldn't say anything to me. But I overheard a couple of them, and they said something that sounded like arson. All that they said to me is they'll know more later."

Christie watched as thick black smoke poured from the windows of Lana's house. "I don't like this one bit. You or the kids could have been seriously hurt or even killed. It makes me wonder how far Erik will go to get revenge on what he thinks you stole from him."

"I'd be careful making assumptions just yet." Mike pushed his hat back off his forehead. "We need all the facts first."

Lana nodded. "True." She burst out crying, and Orchid gathered her up as a mother hen would do with a chick.

"There, there. You let it out." Orchid stroked Lana's hair.

Christie motioned for Mike to step away from the pair. She turned her back from the women and lowered her voice. "What do you think, Mike? Are Lana and the kids in danger?"

"Can't rightly say. But after all y'all told me, I certainly don't like the looks of this. Especially if they're already saying that it looks to be arson." He nodded back toward Lana. "I'll ride with her if that's okay with you and get her settled at Curtis's. Then we'll come over in the morning and pick up my truck."

"That sounds good. I don't like the idea of them being alone. Thanks, Mike."

"Anything for you." He turned and walked back to the women, leaving Christie with a puzzled expression on her face.

~

Morning seemed to arrive too early as Christie's phone dinged with a message, which caused her to pull her pillow over her head. Groaning, she rolled over and pulled the device from her bedside table. It was from Lana.

Lana: Come over. We're fixing pancakes.

The phone dinged again.

Lana: You know you're starving.

Christie's stomach rumbled. Ugh. Even nature was against her sleeping in. She lay back on the bed and debated getting up versus going back to sleep. Finally, she threw off the covers. Padding over to the door, she called out, "Pop, want to go to Curtis's for breakfast?"

No answer. She grabbed her robe off the hook and ambled to the kitchen. He wasn't there. She looked out the window. She couldn't see him out by the stables.

Her phone dinged again.

Lana: Pop says hurry up, he's hungry.

Christie replied that she'd be there soon. She took a quick shower and pulled her wet hair up into a bun. Shucking into a shift dress and flip-flops, she grabbed her keys and headed out the door. Mutt and Jeffrey thumped their tails and grinned broadly. "Okay, you can come." She opened the tailgate, and the pair jumped in the truck bed. As soon as she pulled up, Trey and Allie came running out of the house, only to be attacked with big slobbery dog kisses. Screaming with joy, they ran off toward the side of the house, the dogs running alongside them.

Inside the kitchen, everyone was sitting around the table with coffees while Mike fried up bacon, and Lana prepared pancakes. Mike turned toward her. "Morning."

Pop huffed. "It's almost afternoon."

"Pop, it's only ten in the morning, that's certainly not afternoon. Plus, we didn't go to bed until after four this morning." She accepted a cup of coffee from Curtis. "Thanks, much appreciated and needed."

Curtis sat down in the seat next to Christie. "Mike and Lana have been telling us all about the fire. God was watching over her and them young-un's last night."

"I'll feel better when the Fire Marshall comes back with his report. Then we'll know what happened. But if it was arson, then it's pretty obvious that someone meant harm."

Mike set down a plate of bacon and sausages. "Best to wait to hear everything before jumping to conclusions."

Lana finished the batch of pancakes and joined the others at the table. "True. We don't know if it was a terrible accident or on purpose. Even if it were, what's the reason for it? I barely know anyone here."

"But with you out of the picture, maybe Erik thinks he still gets Curtis to part with more land." Christie poured some maple syrup on her pancakes.

"He'd be stupid to try something like that. He'd be the first suspect." Lana added a couple of pancakes to her plate.

Pop swallowed before declaring, "Well, he ain't the sharpest tool in the tool shed." Turning to face Christie, he said, "I'm thinking your coming home has jinxed us." He winked at her.

"Funny. I can't help it that you all have greedy and horrible people in your midst. People can fool you. It just shows that lots of people here may be too gullible about others."

A quiet settled over the room. Mike had undergone a divorce because of being deceived.

"Oh, sorry, Mike. I didn't—"

"Nope, you're right. Maybe my radar isn't as good on determining the good people versus the bad folks." He wiped his mouth and stood. "Excuse me." He walked out of the kitchen and they heard the screen at the front door slam.

"You go apologize to him," Pop intoned.

"Pop, I'm not a kid. I already said I was sorry, but yes, I'll go speak to him." She put her napkin on the seat and walked outside to the bench where Mike sat.

"I'm sorry, Mike. I shouldn't have said that." She sighed and waved at the seat. "May I?"

He shrugged. "If you don't mind sitting next to a fool."

"You're not a fool. I was fooled too, remember. Trust me; I shouldn't judge you or anyone. Since coming back here, it's been a real wake-up call about people. I think I had these rose-colored glasses on that once I moved home, life would be perfect. It's been anything but."

"There is no 'perfect.' There's good, and there're moments of joy and sorrow. But amid all of it, there's simply being content and happy."

"True. I guess these last months have made me leerier of everyone, and to be honest, untrustworthy of everyone and their agenda."

"I hear you. I've felt the same way. Even at work, they've commented on my changed attitudes but stopped after I gave them grief about it." He leant over and put his elbows on his thighs. "I think I'm tired. Tired of being away from Jess. Tired of the oilfield life. Just plain ol' tired."

"Friends again?" Christie held out her hand.

"Christie—" He stopped and gazed into her eyes.

Butterflies bounced in her stomach. She sprung up from the bench. "I'm so glad we're friends, Mike. I could use a friend. And so could Lana. We need to be there for her. I hope that soon she'll find a good man like you and maybe marry again."

He stood. "Lana's a great gal. But she's a kid to me. Like a baby sister. So I hope you're not thinking that we can be together."

Christie smiled. "No, I just, I mean—"

"Friends then." He held out his hand.

CHAPTER NINE

The sound of footsteps on gravel caused them to turn to the source. It was Erik.

"You've got some nerve." Christie strode toward him. "I guess you don't realize that a closed gate means 'keep out.' What are you doing here?"

"Listen, we got off on a very wrong foot. I admit I saw dollar signs. My business was struggling financially, and I needed an influx of capital. But after that happened, I sold a piece of property in Dallas."

Christie's eyes narrowed, and she breathed deeply. No way was he telling the truth. What did he have up his sleeve?

"Look, I can tell you don't believe me. I get it. But I'm here, and I'm admitting I behaved badly."

"So that's why you're here? Okay, you'd said your piece. I'll let Curtis know."

Erik brushed his hand through his hair and finally acknowledged Mike. "Sorry." He held out his hand. "I don't think we've met. I'm Erik."

"I'm Jess's dad."

"Youch. Listen. He jumped on me. I was only defending myself. Plus, I didn't know he was a kid."

"I don't see how that matters, seeing as you were already trespassing on the Taylor's property."

Erik stared at Mike. "Like I told her, I didn't start the fire in the barn. When I saw it, that's when I went in, and she confronted me."

Christie bristled. "I *confronted* you!"

"Look, this isn't the way I planned. I shouldn't have been on your property. That's true. I'll give you that. I wanted to see your house in relation to where the land dipped down. It's hard to get a real feel by a blueprint or even a maps app. I expected to just see the area, go through the fence opening and get back onto Curtis's property. When I saw the fire in the barn, that's when I came over."

"What do you mean fence opening?" Christie crossed her arms.

"There's an opening between the two fences. It's a fairly good size. I figured it was to take the horses through to your place."

Mike interrupted. "Okay, I'll give you that it may have been a misunderstanding. I may have done the same thing if I'd had someone jump on me. But that doesn't excuse the fact that you threatened Christie and I won't abide by that."

Erik raised his hands. "Again, not trying to stir up trouble. I came to apologize to Curtis for my behavior, but I also need to speak to him about something important."

"You can tell me, and I'll tell him."

"No. I want Curtis to be the first to hear what I have to say."

The trio stood in silence before Christie nodded. "Okay, but you wait here. I'll go get Curtis."

Christie went inside and returned with Curtis, Pop, and Lana. Mike and Erik had moved over into the shade of the oak grove, each eyeing the other warily.

Erik stepped forward as Lana approached. "Hello. I gather you're Lana. I don't think we've been formally introduced." He held out his hand, which Lana took.

"Hello."

Pop and Curtis had sat down on the bench, and the others stood around, waiting. Finally Erik spoke. "I apologize. First to Curtis. Then to all of you. I regret the way I acted. But I had nothing to do with the barn fire." He turned to Lana. "Blood may not relate us, but tragedy relates us. We've both lost someone tragically."

"Lana's father was murdered." Christie moved next to the young woman.

Erik turned to Curtis. "Someone murdered Nick."

"What?" Curtis grabbed the arm of the bench.

"Received the call yesterday. After the autopsy and toxicology reports came back, they determined Nick died from a combination of opioids, not carbon monoxide."

"Well, he could have done that to ensure his death."

Erik shook his head. "I know Nick. He would barely take an aspirin for a headache. He would have had to go to a doctor to get a prescription. It doesn't fit. However, the problem was that there was no pill bottle found in the car. He would have needed to uncap all the pills and dissolve them in the whiskey. Here's the thing—" He started pacing. "Why do that at all? If you want to take the pills, then just swallow them and chase them with the whiskey. Plus, there wasn't that much alcohol in his system. That means all the pills needed to be in those first few swallows. And here's the clincher. Only his fingerprints and DNA were on the bottle."

"Well, of course they were. He was the one drinking it." Lana retorted.

"But he had to have bought it. The store clerk's fingerprints should be on it. Someone had to have wiped the bottle clean and then pressed it to his hand."

Christie's mind whirled. Who would have killed Nick and why would he be at Curtis's house? She'd never understood why he had driven himself out to the ranch.

Erik was still talking, "They've determined cause of death is suspicious—undetermined. Anyway, I wanted to tell you in person. If it turns out to be true, that Nick didn't kill himself—"

"Then he didn't kill my father." Lana whispered.

~

Once Erik left, the group sat around the kitchen table, each going over the last few months. Christie spoke. "I think Erik's trying to—"

"Could be. Don't like that fella." Mike responded.

Pop slammed his hand on the table. "How 'bout you all speak in complete sentences and no mind-reading needed."

"If I'm thinking what Christie's thinking, Erik is trying to cover his a—." Mike glanced at her.

"Exactly. Think about it. If he killed Nick, no need to split the profits. Now that they're looking at this as possible murder versus suicide, then he has to act as if he's as surprised as we are. He has to look contrite in order to get us to be on his side."

Lana turned from the sink, where she'd been washing up the breakfast dishes. "Does this mean that he may have killed my father? He seems so nice."

"That's what they always say about the guy *after* he murders his entire family. 'But he was so nice.' We're going to have to stick to the facts." Christie counted off with her fingers. "Erik admits he was in trouble financially. Two, he and Nick wanted to get Curtis to sell the property. As that grew more unlikely, Erik got desperate. Three, then your dad comes along and puts an even bigger kink in the works. All we know is that someone killed your dad and tried to frame Curtis. That didn't work. Then, Nick dies. Now, we find out his death is suspicious. Who benefits from both deaths? Erik."

"Well, technically that could also be me. I inherit after my father, and with Nick gone, the only issue is getting Curtis to sell his land. So instead, I just move in here!" Lana wiped her hands on a dry dishtowel.

"But there's still the fire. If you would have been home, we would be holding your funeral now too." Christie folded her hands and tucked them under her chin.

"All I know is I wouldn't trust that man as far as I could throw him." Pop rubbed his mustache and beard. "I'm setting up a shooting area on the back property. Christie, I want you to practice more."

Christie rolled her eyes. "Pop, I took the lessons and got my license to carry. I promise I'll go to Apache and practice if it will make you feel better."

"It will." He patted her hand. "Someone has evil intent and acts on it."

Lana whispered, "I hope it's not Erik."

"Why?" Christie responded.

Lana threw the towel over her shoulder. "Well, he is kind of cute."

"Seriously?"

"Yes." Lana shrugged. "What's wrong with saying that?"

Mike stretched. "Well, I have to go pick up Jess in a bit, and we're going down to the Forum to catch a movie. Christie, can you take me to get my truck?"

"Yes, sure." She hugged Lana. "I'll come back later to help you with the room. I need to work with the horses for a while." She kissed Pop on the top of his head and gave Curtis a peck on the cheek. "See ya after-while."

"So, what do you think?" Mike asked Christie when they were in the truck.

"I don't know. It's hard to believe someone you speak to face-to-face could be a cold-blooded killer."

"I don't get a sense of anything with Erik. Other than I wanted to have a go at him for harming my son."

"That's probably pretty natural, I would think."

Mike's phone rang. It was Jess. He listened and then spoke. "That's fine." He disconnected the call. "He's in the middle of a game with his friends, so he wants to stay longer. Actually, I think it's more because of a young lady named Sarah. Ah, puppy love."

"It may be puppy love, but it sure is real to that puppy."

Mike chuckled. "True. I can remember those days. I guess that leaves me with free time. You want help with the stalls?"

"That would be great. You sure you're okay working on your day off?"

"I'm all yours."

As Christie parked her truck in the back, she turned to Mike. "Do you ride? The more I think about what Erik said, the more I want to find out what he's talking about."

"Sure. I can go start getting the horses ready, and you can change into jeans and boots."

They walked over to the paddock, and Champ walked up to her. "This is Champ. He's my horse—Oh geez, of course, you know him." Champ had been Mike's wife's horse, but she'd given Champ to Christie.

"It's fine." Mike pointed to a gelding out toward the back of a larger paddock. "Who's that fine fella? He's a good-looking male."

The Paint stared at them from across the field.

Christie shielded her eyes with her hand. "That's Scout. He's pretty much a loner. Doesn't like people much. Curtis has been watching him, as his owners are looking to sell him."

Mike made a clicking sound out of the side of his mouth. The horse's ears moved, and he began walking toward Mike.

"What in the—?"

Mike looked at her. "Didn't I tell you? I'm a horse whisperer." He winked at her, causing her cheeks to blush.

The horse approached and stood a few yards from the fence. Mike spoke to the horse in a calm, gentle manner. "I hear you. You came this far. Only fair I come the rest of the way." In one quick movement, Mike mounted the fence and dropped into the paddock. "What do you say, Scout? Friends?" Mike waited for the horse to approach him. Once he did, Mike stroked the Paint's dappled neck. "You're a handsome fella. How about a ride today?" He turned to Christie. "Okay to take Scout out as my ride?"

"I guess. This is crazy. He doesn't take to anyone. He's okay with Pop, and he tolerates me and Jess."

"Will he be okay with Champ?"

"Yes, they're like two old bachelors. They get along fine when they're together."

"Okay, go change, and I'll get him ready."

By the time Christie arrived back out at the barn, Mike had placed the saddle on Scout. She heard Champ stomping around, ready to get out too. Once Champ was brushed and saddled, they let the horses run. Christie sensed the power as the two males challenged each other for first position. After they'd had a good run, they moved them into an easy canter. As they approached the rocky outcropping Erik had spoken of, they dismounted, leading the horses by the reins.

"I don't see what Erik was talking about. The fence line is fine."

Mike replied, "Let's leave the horses here and get a closer look." They took the horses over to a shade tree and secured them there.

As Christie made her way down the rocky shelf, Mike took her hand and helped her down to the flat area. The fence looked intact.

"Maybe Erik meant somewhere else. But he said the area close to where I'm going to build my house."

Mike walked on ahead and motioned for Christie to follow. "Come look at this."

As Christie drew closer, she noticed one fence section out from the other. Looking at it straight on, it appeared to be another fence section. Yet there was an opening in between the two fences, adequate for a horse and rider to pass through it easily.

"Wow. I need to ask Curtis about this. I didn't think we had an opening between the properties, but this doesn't look new."

Mike checked the posts of both fences. "Someone could have designed them to look as close as possible."

"Well, that certainly explains that rider."

"What rider?"

"When I first visited Pop, there was an incident where a fire started in the kitchen. Luckily, I arrived home in time. I think Pop left a frying pan with grease in it on the stove, and I had a hard time waking him, so that's probably why he didn't smell the smoke. Anyway, when I opened the back door, I saw someone astride a horse. I didn't know how they'd gotten onto our property. I guess now I know."

"Wouldn't they have to come from Curtis's property? How could they have done that without him seeing?"

"I don't know. But we need to do something here."

"How about I put up a gate you can lock?"

"Mike, you don't—"

"Y'all are letting Jess stay here so he can finish high school. That means a lot to him and to me. So let me help with this."

"Okay, I accept your generous offer."

"Well, it may have to be the next time I'm here. I have to return to the oilfield tomorrow. Will that be okay?"

"Yes." It was the first time Christie realized she hated the idea Mike would leave.

CHAPTER TEN

After they'd brushed down the horses and picked out their hooves, they led the horses to a farther paddock with a large water trough and shaded areas. A few other horses were grazing on some grasses. They walked back to the house, and Christie's phone dinged with a text message.

Lana: Emma and Tyler are here. Can you come?

Christie: Be there in ten.

Christie thanked Mike for all his help and jumped in the truck. She wanted a cool shower, but it had to wait. Arriving at the Altgelt ranch, Christie spied Emma and Tyler up on the porch with Curtis and Lana. As she approached, Christie noted the mottled bruising on Emma's face and her arm in a soft cast.

"What happened to you?" Christie pointed to her arm.

"Um, I…" She fumbled. "Clumsy. Fell at home and—
"

"We should sue you." Tyler ignored Christie and spoke to Lana. Christie made her way quickly to Lana's side. Emma turned to him with a stunned expression.

"For what? I didn't start the fire." Lana bristled.

"That is a rental property. We're going to be losing revenue now. Awful convenient that you're moving out when this happens."

"It wasn't awfully convenient for Lana to lose all her furnishings or belongings. She, along with her children, could have lost their lives. If anyone needs to sue, it's Lana." Christie crossed her arms over her chest.

Emma broke down crying, ignoring Tyler's glare. "It's so awful. I can't imagine. We always have smoke detectors in all our properties. Maybe the battery hadn't been changed or… anyway, I'm sorry you lost everything."

"Thankfully, not everything. I'd already packed my van with personal items."

Christie noted a strange look pass over Tyler's face.

Emma sniffed. "Oh good. Of course, we have no intention of suing." She made a quick glance toward Tyler. "We're just thankful that all of you are safe. It looks like the front facade can be saved, and that house was tiny. Now, we can expand on it and make it bigger, so we may actually end up better for future rental potential. We wanted to see how you're doing and to let you know you're welcome to see if there's anything salvageable. No more rent monies are due, and I'm returning your check for this month." Using two fingers of her injured hand, she plucked a check from her purse and handed it to Lana.

"Thanks. This will come in handy to replace furniture. I don't think Dad or Mom had rental insurance." Lana folded the check and stuck it in her jeans pocket.

Curtis spoke up. "I think y'all have done said your piece."

"Um, yes." Emma cradled her arm as she turned away. As her eyes met Christie's, Emma ducked her head and spoke. "Well, goodbye." She gingerly made her way down the steps and toward the truck. Tyler opened the door, and Emma pulled herself up into the cab with her left hand. Backing out of the drive, Curtis said, "She doesn't deserve him."

"I agree, Curtis."

Lana looked back and forth between them. "What do you mean? I don't think he's very nice."

"That's exactly what we mean. She's a decent person. He runs hot and cold. We've seen that a few times now. I don't believe for a second that the bruises and injury to her arm and hand were accidents. She may have fallen, but it was probably because someone pushed her." Christie sighed. "Well, I'm here and already dirty and sweaty from riding, might as well help you a bit."

Curtis tipped his hat. "Great. I'm off for some important business. You gals have fun."

Christie laughed. "You mean coffee and dominoes with the guys?"

"Exactly."

After Curtis left, Lana showed Christie to Allie's room. Lana had painted one wall a bright pink, and there were paper flowers taped to the wall. "Watch this." Lana removed the paper, and underneath were daisy petals. As she pulled off the centerpiece, Christie leaned in. "That almost looks like it's smiling."

"It is. Orchid helped me with this. The kids said what they wanted, along with colors, then she created this, so all I had to do was follow instructions. They haven't seen this yet, as I'm keeping them as a surprise for now." Lana opened the door across the hall. Instead of being light and bright like Allie's, this one was dark blue with constellations and planets.

"Impressive. Where are they sleeping, then?"

Lana gestured down the hall. "We're bunking in here right now. I'd planned to bring the bunk beds over soon. Looks like I'll be going for bed shopping first." She shut the door and then proceeded to the large master bedroom. Things had been removed from the room, and it now contained paint equipment, ladders, a shop-vac, and other odds and ends. "My goal today is to remove this old popcorn ceiling. You up for it?"

Christie replied by twisting her hair up in a tight bun. "Let's do this." They worked until it was time for Lana to pick up the kids from martial arts.

"Thanks. I appreciate the help." She gave Christie a hug. "And I don't just mean working on this room. I mean with everything. Handling Erik, the Websters, it's been one thing after another."

"That's what friends do."

"Yes, but I feel you all have become more than friends. You're like the extended family I've always wanted." She cocked her head. "I hope that doesn't sound too cheesy?"

"Who doesn't love cheese?" Christie grinned. "Listen, I had Jess pick up the owl and take it over to Orchid's. I thought with Orchid's eye for detail, maybe she could help us see if there's anything about that owl or if it was simply something your dad said."

"Oh, I want to come too. I can see if there is anything salvageable at the house. The front took the brunt of it, but the kitchen and back bedroom might have things I can save."

"Okay. Let me call Orchid and see what time works for her." Christie dialed Orchid's number and, after a short conversation, ended the call. "She says come around eleven, and she'll prepare brunch."

"Yum. That sounds great."

The following morning, Christie and Lana drove down to Orchid's.

Orchid's door was painted black. It was the first time that Christie had seen a color that wasn't cheerful. As she walked toward the door, she saw that one spot in the upper right was bright white, and light streaks off it emanated out onto the other part. Lana had pulled up, so Christie waited for her to join her. "That's interesting. Wait." Lana stood on her tiptoes, and before Christie knew what was happening, tears were streaming down Lana's face. "Orchid is the best, kindest..."

Christie looked up at the area where Lana had focused. As she moved her head, she noticed that it was actually more of a flat and glossy white in varying tones. Within the middle was a simple word, "Hope."

"Oh my gosh, even in the darkness—"

Lana finished it. "There's a glimmer of hope."

The door opened with Orchid dressed in a bright yellow top with red polka dotted capris, "Are you two going to stand there all day or coming in?"

Lana flew over to the woman. "Oh, Miz Merryweather." She tucked her head and hugged the woman.

"Child, you know it's only the special ones that get so much grief. You'll make it through this and be all the stronger for it." She reached over and grasped Christie's hand. "Now come inside." She led them through her living room, which held lots of partitions like you'd see in an office.

"What in the—?"

"Come on. Follow me." They walked past prints of various artists with similar styles to Esher. When they'd exited the short maze and entered the opening to the kitchen, Orchid raised a finger to her lips. "Say nothing. Don't think about it. Just let it be."

Christie stifled a chuckle. If you looked up eccentric in the dictionary, it had to have Orchid's picture there. She'd heard about artists but this was the first time she'd dealt with someone so…she struggled for a word, then settled on unique.

"Now, let's eat. I've set up a place for us out back. Just let me pull this quiche from the oven."

After Orchid handed the quiche to Christie, she took up a bowl of fruit and had Lana carry a container of potatoes and grilled veggies.

After they'd enjoyed the meal, Orchid said, "Okay, now you can ask me about the front room."

Christie wiped her mouth with a napkin. "Not really sure what to ask. I know you decorate it differently all the time, but this was… um, distinctive."

Orchid turned to Lana. "And what did you think?"

"It reminded me of those mirrored mazes in the funhouses I used to enjoy when I was a kid."

"That's it exactly. What did you think of the artwork? And you, Christie?"

"It's Esher, correct? You stare at it and see one thing, but if you look at it another way, you get a different perspective. Is that what we need to do with the owl?"

"Yes. I looked at the owl like you all had done. I knew most of the time they showed it from the front. You had told me that you'd seen it up on a shelf so it wasn't something that could be seen that way." She rose. "Come on. I think it's better if I show you."

The trio went back inside. The owl sat on a counter. Orchid walked in front and, skimming the counter with her hand, knocked a bunch of papers to the floor. "Here, let me get those for you." Christie bent to her knees and picked up the papers. She glanced up at the owl. "Oh, my gosh."

"What?" Lana moved over to Christie. "What is it? I don't see anything."

"Here. Get on your knees next to me."

Lana joined Christie. "Oh wow. It's the wing. There's like an outline." She stood up. "What do you think it means?"

Orchid tapped her manicured white fingernail to her temple. "I *know* what it means."

She took the papers from Christie. "It was the ear that did it. Look here. It was damaged at some point. However, because there's so much detail, it looks more like a part of the ear. Here's my hypothesis on what occurred. I think maybe your father stumbled, and as he did, the owl tipped, causing the ear to scratch. When he put the owl back, he must have turned it so that the owl's side was clear. I gather when he stumbled, he probably did what I just had you do, pick up some dropped papers. He noticed the area, and that's when he found this." With a swift movement, Orchid touched something on the inner wing and the base, and they heard a click. Carefully, she moved the wing back to reveal a cavity inside the statue.

"Whoa. That's awesome."

Christie leaned over to look. "What's inside?"

"That's the issue. Whatever was inside here is gone. Someone took it."

"So we know Tyler wanted the owl. Maybe he was using it like a safe." Lana proposed.

"Could be. Maybe he went to that lady's house to retrieve what was inside, and her death really was an accident."

Lana bit her cheek. "Or Erik got it for him. They are buddy-buddy."

"I don't know. We have no idea what was in there. I'm not sure Tyler would ask Erik to do that."

"Maybe that's why Erik went there. He could have kept her busy while Tyler looked at the owl." Lana shifted her position.

"Or Emma. He could have told her she needed to distract the woman while he looked at the owl."

"That's interesting, Christie. What do you think, Orchid?"

"Not for me to say."

Christie harrumphed. "Why, if you don't think that Erik or Tyler—" She stopped, her mouth opening in surprise.

Orchid nodded.

"What is it? I don't get what you two are thinking." Lana huffed.

Christie lowered her voice. "Your father. Your father found it."

CHAPTER ELEVEN

They left Orchid's after cleaning up the dishes, and Christie went over to the house across the street. They walked to the back and entered through the kitchen.

"Most of this was Mom's stuff. She took what she wanted, so I'm not sure there's anything worth keeping." She stepped over debris and made her way into the living room. This area's destruction was complete, and she picked her way gingerly to the short hallway. The front bedroom was not unlike the living room, and the back bedroom appeared to be fairly intact. However, on closer inspection, the area had been soaked by the fire department. Lana shook her head. "Oh well. I do think I may be able to retrieve some of our clothes. I'll come back later when I have on work stuff and bring some bags and boxes." They exited the house.

"What's the rest of the day's agenda?"

"I've got some errands to run, and then I'll be picking the kids up from school today. Curtis helped me finish the ceiling, so I'll start painting today or tomorrow. Need to get this done even quicker now that I'm moving in sooner than I'd planned."

Christie unlocked her truck. "I can't today. I'm going down to the architect's offices to finalize the plans. Won't be long before we'll break ground."

"I saw the huge stack of logs. Impressive."

"Yes, we hired some guys to come out and cut back the cedar we could use for the project. It's also opened up the land too. There's more space to ride and the cleared space makes me think we may be able to put in a water-catchment pond."

"A what?"

"I've been reading a book on permaculture. Pretty interesting about creating food forests and such. I don't have the inclination to grow crops, but it'd be nice to have a small garden. I met the author when I stayed at her bed-and-breakfast in Colorado."

"Maybe I'll look into it after I'm done with all my current studies."

"How's that coming?"

Lana groaned. "I may be too old for this. I already have something like ten books I have to get, and they're like a car payment. So expensive."

"It will be worth it. You'll be glad you did it once it's said and done." Christie started the truck with her remote start. "Plus, if you're old, what does that make me?"

"Ancient." Lana grinned.

"I see how it is. And after I said I'd help paint too. This is the thanks I get." She climbed into the truck.

"See ya later, granny." Lana waved.

Christie stuck out her tongue and Lana broke out laughing.

The pair spent the next few days painting the master bedroom and attached master bath, working long into the night. In the evenings, Jess would come over and help the kids with their homework or keep them entertained. Because of the fire, Lana had found an old bed frame that she'd stripped and painted with an antique cream glaze. She'd lured some of Jess's friends into helping move furniture into the rooms with the lure of pizza, sodas, and some cash.

Christie came over for coffee the next morning. "Wow, this all looks great. I bet the kids were happy finally getting to be in their rooms."

"Yes, I can't wait until things settle down a bit. I know the first semester will be the hardest, but at least it's while the kids are in school."

"We should plan something fun for this coming weekend. I mean, Curtis and Pop are already on their way to the coast again. What do you think?"

"What about the kids?"

"Allie is at a birthday sleep over on Friday, and I'm sure I could get Jess to watch Trey."

"I'll think about it. What do you have in mind?"

"Dinner on the Riverwalk or take in a show?"

"That could be a plan. So what now?"

Lana motioned for Christie to follow her back to the kitchen. "This."

"Are you crazy?"

"I already received permission from Curtis. He said I could do whatever I wanted. The kitchen isn't bad; it just needs a good scrubbing down, a bit more organization, and a fresh coat of paint. We already agreed on this one." Lana showed Christie a butter-cream yellow. "I also plan to make some valances out of this." She pulled some fabric out of a bag. Unfolding the fabric, Christie saw red strawberries with a green buffalo-checked border.

"That's cute and cheerful."

The wall phone rang, and Lana picked it up. "Hello?" she responded to the caller. "No, sorry, he's not in and won't be back until next week. Can I take a message?" She shifted her shoulder to keep the phone to her ear. "Okay, thanks."

Lana hung up the phone in the cradle. "Must be a telemarketer. They never want to leave a message." She folded the fabric back in the bag and moved it out of the way. The pair spent the rest of the day cleaning and organizing the cabinets so that Lana would have room for her items.

Later, as they took a break, Christie told Lana about the opening in the fence. "Hmmm. I would definitely tell Curtis about it when he gets home." She lifted her soda and took a swig. "I've been thinking about that owl. Do you think my dad found something he shouldn't have?"

"I think he found the development plans for this place. I also believe he meant to tell Curtis but figured he'd have another opportunity."

"As sad as it all is, I'm glad my dad finally got to meet his father, no matter how brief." Her face grew crimson, and a tear slid down her cheek. "I miss him so much. I want to see him get justice."

"I can understand that. Let's get to work; otherwise, my 'get-up-and-go' may get up and go take a nap!"

They finished cleaning the kitchen and decided to paint early the next morning. The day passed quickly. In the afternoon, they stopped work so Lana could get the kids ready to go for the evening, and Christie headed home to get ready for their night out. Christie put on a denim broom skirt and an orange top with copper and brown accents. At the last minute, she added a new accessory and then slipped into a pair of woven Huaraches she'd picked up during a trip into San Antonio.

Arriving over at the Altgelt Ranch, Christie knocked on the open door. "Hello!"

"I'm back here. Come on back to my room."

"Okay. Want me to shut this door?"

"No. It's fine. Trying to air out the paint smell some. The windows aren't doing it." Christie noticed the box fan in the corner going full-speed. She walked to the master and found Lana in front of a closet. "Sorry, running a bit late, what with the kids and all."

"You dog. You took a nap, didn't you?"

Lana held her hands up. "Guilty as charged."

"I'll remember that the next time you call me old."

"How hot do you think it'll be?" She pulled her hair up into her hands. "It'll only take me a minute to dress, but I don't want to be too hot."

"This is Texas. We have sort of hot, hot, hotter, and hot as Hades."

"Okay." Lana grabbed a brush. "Up it is." She turned to Christie. "Would you like me to put your hair up in a French braid?"

"That'd be great."

"Okay, let me finish. Then, I'll work on yours."

As Lana worked on her hair, Christie looked around the room. "You got a lot more done. I love how you've decorated the room." She went over to a side table where a marquetry box sat on it. "This is beautiful."

"Thanks. My dad gave it to me. He said it could hold my wishes and dreams or jewelry. Whichever made more sense."

"Sounds like a great guy."

"He was. Can you hand it to me? I've put a necklace in there that I want to wear tonight."

Christie handed it to her, but Lana turned at the last minute. "Did you hear that?"

The box slipped from Christie's hands and bounced on the carpet. Jewelry flew out, and a mirror inside the top fell out onto the carpet.

"Oh, Lana, sorry. I thought you had it."

"No worries. It should go right back in." She bent down and picked up the box and the mirror while Christie gathered the jewelry. When Christie rose, she noticed an odd look on Lana's face.

"What is it?"

Lana turned the box toward Christie. A thick, nine-inch manila envelope was crammed into the space behind where the mirror had been. With shaking hands, Lana pulled it out and opened it. She dumped the contents onto the table. It was a smaller thick envelope, a passport, and a folded sheet of paper. Lana unfolded the paper.

She covered her mouth with her hand. "It's a letter from my dad."

"What does it say?"

Lana sat down in the chair next to the table. "It says, 'If you're reading this, I'm no longer alive. Know I love you all.' K." She handed the letter to Christie.

"Look at this." She handed the passport to Christie. Inside it revealed information for Jeff Collins, but the picture was that of Tyler Webster.

Christie paced the floor. "What in the—?"

"This envelope contains various IDs and credit cards, all under the name Jeff Collins. Plus a lot of cash. I'd say at least a thousand or more in hundreds." She twisted in her seat. "You think this is what Dad found in the owl?"

"I wouldn't doubt it. It makes sense."

"This is weird." Lana was looking at another document.

"What is it?"

"A birth certificate. But this one says Dan Lord."

She stood up to hand the document to Christie when they heard a sound. Tyler stood in the door. "Glad you found that. I'll take those back now."

Lana lunged for the poker next to the fireplace. She held it tightly with both hands like a sword in front of her.

Tyler laughed. "What are you, two feet and eighty pounds soaking wet? I've taken on bigger fish than you." His voice grew husky.

"You mean like my father?"

"That was too bad. I liked your old man. But—" He shook his head "—he shouldn't have meddled. I realized that he wouldn't be bought. Hate those religious types, all faith and doing what's right," he rambled on. "He even tried to get me to 'do the right thing. '"

Christie stood frozen. Her mind racing.

Lana waved the poker and took a step back. "So you killed him. Not Nick."

"Ahh, Nick. Another guy with a change of heart." He sighed. "These people. I had him call Kurt out to the house so they could talk. But I went earlier. Your dad was always early. Then I convinced Nick that they would consider him an accessory after the fact. He tried to get Erik to back out of our deal. I couldn't have that. He agreed, but he was a loose cannon."

"So you were going to frame him, and he killed himself." Lana tightened her grip on the poker.

Christie spoke. "No, he killed Nick and made it look that way."

He laughed. "Ding, ding, ding. We have a winner. Two birds, one stone. I couldn't have planned it better. I told him we'd reached a deal and offered him the first shot. Then, I waited until he became groggy. People shouldn't mess with me and think they can get away with it."

He took a step into the room, eyeing the pair. "I think you first." He pointed to Lana, who was now shaking with the weight of the poker. She clenched and unclenched it in her hands.

"Curtis and his friends will be back in any minute. We'll give you a chance to turn yourself in."

Tyler acted like he was dialing a phone and then spoke in a different voice. "Oh, he's not there. No message. We'll call back next week."

He took another step, and Lana raised the poker like a bat.

"Ahh, that's cute." He pulled a knife from his belt. He waved it between the pair. "Let's see, eany, meany …"

Lana raised the poker up. "I will kill you."

He burst out laughing. "I don't think so."

"I will." He turned to face Christie as she pulled her pistol from the Dene Adam's thigh holster.

"You won't use that."

"I wouldn't bet on that. The first thing I learned is 'be ready to shoot to kill.' I am. Now, drop the knife."

He hesitated, and Christie's training kicked in high gear. She racked the slide. "Now!"

He dropped the knife, and she motioned with the gun for him to move away from it. When he stepped away, Lana sprang over and grabbed it. Christie said, "Now on your knees, hands behind your head. Slowly. One false move and this gun goes off. I have no qualms of shooting you."

As he knelt down, Lana dialed 9-1-1. She explained what had happened, and that Christie had a weapon trained on Tyler.

Time slowed to a crawl. Finally, they heard the wailing of sirens and the shouts of men yelling, "Sheriff's Department."

Men entered with guns drawn. Sheriff Clauson came in and went up to Christie, whose grip was locked on the gun. In a soothing voice, he said, "We got this, Christie. You can put the weapon down."

The deputy's put Tyler in cuffs and took him out of the house. Clauson took the gun from Christie and handed it to a nearby deputy. Christie broke down in tears, shaking. "I… I think I'm going to be sick."

She sprinted to the bathroom. After washing her face and drying off her hands, she emerged to a team of EMTs and a victim's advocate who had wrapped Lana in a thick quilt and were speaking softly to her. The EMTs checked Christie and then loaded up their gear.

Lana saw Christie and sprang up into an embrace. "I thought we were going to die. I kept thinking I'll never see my children again." Tears streamed down both of their faces.

"Not so bad for an old lady, huh?" Christie grinned.

CHAPTER TWELVE

Christie had gone with a deputy back to the house to grab an overnight bag. As she left, Mutt and Jeffrey wagged their tails. "Yes, you guys can come too." They bounded up into the truck bed. Lana and Christie spent a sleepless night, watching comedy movies, jumping at every sound, but soothed because neither of the dogs rallied from their slumber at their feet.

As the morning sun tore away the shadows of the room, they woke from sleep as Pop and Curtis drove up to the house. Christie ran outside and grabbed Pop's neck and hugged him tight. "Pop, I'm so glad you're here."

"Darlin', shush. It's okay." He wiped her tears. "It's okay now."

Everyone went into the kitchen and sat around the table while Christie composed herself. "I'm so glad you made me take those lessons. Never, ever in a million years, would I think I'd ever need it."

"You never want to hear a smoke detector go off either, but it's important to have one. Always say, best to be prepared. In this case, it probably saved your lives."

Lana held up the coffeepot, and everyone nodded assent. "When did you get that thigh holster?"

"After you showed me the corset one, I went online to check them out. Anna Taylor has lots of videos, and when I saw that women of all sizes could wear it, I thought I'd try it." She sat back in the chair. "The funny thing is that I hadn't planned on it. I knew we'd be doing a lot of walking, and unlike you young skinny things, our thighs can rub together."

Pop held up his hands. "NPC."

"What?"

"You know, not in polite conversation."

"Pop, you mean TMI?"

"TMI, NPC, ABC, who cares."

Christie and Lana shared a glance. "Anyway, I put it on and figured this would be a good time to try it out." She waited to continue until Lana set down cups and poured the coffee. "To be honest, I had planned on removing it before we left to go downtown—"

"Why in tarnation would you do that?" Pop groaned.

Christie held up her hands. "Again, I was getting used to it. In fact, when Tyler came in and threatened us, I'd totally forgotten I had it on me. Thankfully, all that practice kicked in when it was needed."

"I'm just grateful you are both okay." Curtis reached over and took Lana and Christie's hands. "Thank you, Lord, for watching over my girls."

A knock on the door caused Christie to spring from her chair. "Sorry, still a bit jumpy." She spoke to Curtis. "Plus, the point of a gate is so people can't surprise you like that."

"I didn't shut it, as the Sheriff called me and said he was coming out here." Lana went to the door and escorted Sheriff Clauson into the house.

"Hug—" Curtis gestured, "—you hungry? I'm thinking 'bout some biscuits and gravy."

The sheriff removed his hat and set it on a hat hook. "Sounds mighty good to me."

As Lana and Curtis worked on fixing breakfast, Clauson brought them up to date on Tyler. "He lawyered up right away. Not saying anything."

"Will he be released?" A shiver went down Christie's spine.

"Don't expect so. Not since you said you'd press charges. But you never know about these things. We've got him on trespassing, attempted assault with a deadly weapon, forgery, and some other minor things."

"Attempted assault? He would have killed us." Christie paced the room. "I don't like this. Did he even say he'd done anything?"

Clauson accepted a cup of coffee and took a swig before continuing. "No. Only that he wanted a lawyer."

Lana put a batch of biscuits in the oven. "When will he go before the judge about bail?"

"Not sure, but I doubt he'll come back here. Though, always good to remain vigilant."

"Can I talk to him?" Christie wrapped her hands around her mug.

What?" Lana swung around.

"It's just that there are so many unanswered questions. Did he start the fire in Curtis's barn, and what about the cairn in the field? He may have done these horrible things, but we don't know if he had anything to do with the other mishaps, including the fire in our kitchen. I want to talk to him."

"Once this goes through the process, you might visit then. For now, let it take its course." He looked around at the kitchen. "I like what you've done with the place."

"Yes-sirree, it's good having a woman in the house again." Curtis stirred the thick, white gravy.

As they ate breakfast, the conversation turned to the weather, what crops Curtis would plant, and Lana's college courses.

Christie smiled as the group chatted and laughed. The banality of life. It felt like a balm for her heart.

The weeks passed quickly and brought with them the sounds of bulldozers clearing the land for her house. Every day, a new landscape would appear. She'd changed the room orientation so that her bedroom received the morning sun and it would look down onto what she envisioned as her garden. At night, the first hints of the coming cooler months teased at a new season.

She woke to the sound of hammering. "What in the—?" Christie yanked her robe from the hook and padded out to the front where the door stood open.

Mike was outside in the front, a pile of new wood at his feet. He wore a white tee-shirt and jeans. "Oh sorry, did I wake you?"

She mumbled under her breath a 'what does it look like' but forced out an, "I needed to get up soon, anyway." She nodded toward the pile. "What are you doing?"

"Helping Jess with a project." He wiped his brow of sweat.

"I heard you plan on going to see Tyler."

Christie nodded. "I need some answers."

"Mind if I tag along with you?"

"I guess that would be okay. I'm leaving here around one."

"Great. I'll be ready then." He returned to hammering.

Christie closed the door and padded into the kitchen. After pouring a cup of Pop's strong brew, she sipped at it while gazing out at the horses in the back. Suddenly, a mare stamped the ground around her colt. "What in the—?"

Christie shucked into a pair of boots at the back door and ran toward the paddock. Mike, hearing the commotion, had sprinted around the house and they ran over to the horses.

"Stay back!" He put his hand out to Christie. Mike quickly hopped the fence, and Christie realized what was happening. A rattlesnake poised to strike.

"Mike, watch out!" He backed up from the snake but directly into the horse's path as it reared up, knocking Mike to the ground. The snake lay dead as the horse pawed at the ground. Everything moved in slow motion as Christie climbed over the fence and raced over to him. "Mike, Mike!"

She heard a voice yelling out, "Dad!" Jess had raced out of the trailer after hearing all the commotion, the teenager's face in a contortion of fear.

"Jess, call 9-1-1. Hurry!"

"Mike, Mike, can you hear me?" She checked his vitals, but his pulse was weak. She looked down toward his legs. Two torn patches on his jeans made Christie pull up his pants leg. Large marks on his boots showed where the rattlesnake's fangs would have entered.

He roused. "What—?"

"Don't move. I think you may have hit your head when you jumped back from the snake and collided with the horse."

He groaned. "I'm fine. Just got the breath knocked out of me for a minute." He sat up, and dizziness overtook him. "Whoa."

Jess ran out to the paddock in boots and long gym shorts. "Is he okay?" He jumped the fence in one easy movement.

"I think he's fine, but he narrowly escaped being bit by a rattlesnake or stomped to death by a horse. What was he thinking, coming in here?" Tears welled up in her eyes.

"That's my dad. He wouldn't have wanted that snake to get that horse."

When the fire truck arrived, an EMT jumped down with his gear. Seeing Christie, he said, "And we meet again."

"Not because I want to." She moved away from Mike, who could stand on his own after a while. They gave instructions for Christie to monitor him for any concussion symptoms.

Mike grinned. "Well, looks like you're stuck with me now."

Deciding to put off the visit to Tyler until the next day, Christie, Mike, and Jess spent the afternoon watching classic eighties movies on television. Jess slept on and off, waking up every once in a while, to joke about the clothing, hairstyles, or technology. The next day, Christie and Mike headed to the jail where Tyler was being held. After going through screening, Christie and Mike sat in front of Tyler, who wore an orange jumpsuit and flip-flops.

Tyler smirked. "This your lover-boy bodyguard?"

Christie ignored the statement. "I'm here to ask some questions."

"You can ask all you want but doesn't mean I'll have to answer."

"It's nothing to do with the current charges."

Tyler folded his arms over his chest. "Continue. It's not like I have anything better to do."

"I want to know about the fire in Curtis's barn."

"You know the food in here sucks."

"How much?" Mike responded.

Tyler glanced over at him. "How much you got?"

Mike pulled out a twenty from his wallet and waved it.

"I also could use some shampoo, extra socks—"

"Fine." He withdrew a couple of twenties. He motioned to the guard who let him lay the money on the table for Tyler, who stuck it in his pocket.

"Here's the thing. I told Nick and Erik that the best way to get someone to sell was to put a little notion in their head that they were losing their mind."

"Like moving things around from their normal spots." Christie added.

"Yep. So as much as possible, they'd go over when they knew Curtis was out or asleep and move things around in the barn. Whether Nick meant to set the fire, or it was an accident we'll never know." He looked between them. "Anything else?"

"What about the fire at our place?"

"Fire?"

"First, there was an accident in the kitchen and later the fire in the barn." Christie hesitated. "Wait, did you have Erik go over there to make it seem like he started that fire?"

"Why would I want to do that?"

"We paid you to give us answers, not for you to respond with questions. Come on, Christie." Mike rose.

"One more thing." She turned to Tyler. "Did you set up that cairn on the land where Curtis was injured? He could have died if we hadn't found him. Plus, did you start the fire at Lana's too?"

"Do you really expect me to answer that?"

Christie stood. "You just did."

They left, and on the way home, stopped for an early dinner. Dusk was settling in when she drove up to the house. Christie spied Lana's kids running around the yard with Mutt and Jeffrey. "What in the world?"

Off into a cleared area, a large pile of brush and wood had been stacked up into a bonfire. She slammed the truck door shut. "Pop, what's going on?"

"I thought it was time for a good old bonfire." He pointed to the top, and there sat the owl. "Orchid had Jess bring it over to me. It's a sweet gesture, but it sounds like it's only been surrounded by tragedy."

"But, Pop, that's an expensive piece of art."

"Dust to dust, ashes to ashes. It's mine, right? So this is my choice." He handed her a box of matches. "What say you?"

She struck the match.

Thank you for buying this book!

To receive special offers, new releases, bonus content,
fun giveaways, along with news about latest books or coming
series,
Sign up here for my newsletter at https://www.vikkiwalton.com/

I also appreciate it when you leave a review to help determine if
this book is a good read for other readers. Thanks much!

Books by Vikki Walton

Fiction
A Backyard Farming Mystery/Colorado
Chicken Culprit
Cordial Killing
Honey Homicide

A Taylor Texas Mystery
Death Takes A Break
Death Makes A Move
Death Stakes A Claim
Death Bakes A Plan (Upcoming 2020)

Nonfiction

Work Quilting: Piece Together Diverse Income Streams; Live an
Insanely Awesome Life

The Smart Woman's Guide to Travel (guide, planner, and journal
all in one)